The Gathering at AngelFire

Diane L. Keyes

"The splendor of friendship comes in the realization that your friend believes in you and your dreams."

ISBN: 1484970438
ISB-13: 9781484970430

Song Credits

"All You Need is Love"
Written by John Lennon and Paul McCartney

"Yesterday"
Written by Paul McCartney

"Then He Kissed Me"
Written by Jeff Barry, Ellie Greenwich, Phil Spector
Made famous by the Crystals

"Whole Lotta Shakin' Goin On"
Written by Dave Williams and Dave Hall
Made famous by Jerry Lee Lewis

*For Andrew, Thomas, Ryan,
Madisen and Gracelyn*

The five true loves of my life.

Acknowledgements

I must first put Ms. Cynthia Sands at the top of my list, for she is truly a divine gift. She kept me on track and edited this book with a protective watchfulness for the characters. Her unfailing professionalism and principled support, makes me feel like I am the most fortunate writer on the planet.

Because I am a comma queen, Cara Fisher added and subtracted, punctuated, and corrected my errant ways and still managed to say she enjoyed the book. A thousand blessings to you and yours, dear Cara!

The picturesque cover art was created by Molly Jimenez. How she managed to juggle three little ones along with her creative work and turn out something so beautiful is mind boggling. I appreciate both your incredible patience and creativity.

Immense appreciation goes to Beatrice Quesada, Jean Curtis, Judy Woodruff, Terry Fisher, and Wendy Marcot, who were advance readers and supreme supporters. They asked to be readers for this second book and I am humbled by their support. Judy Woodruff has even enrolled her book club! Thank you for your willingness to follow the journeys of these characters.

A grand note of gratitude straight from my heart goes to Reverend Rosella Turner, Kate Alves, Beatrice Grizzel, and Suzann Owings, as women who define the art of encouragement, yet again. How did I get so blessed?

Last but certainly not least, I have to thank the CreateSpace team for their willingness to take the time to respond quickly to every question in the publishing process. They must take classes in "*Handholding for Authors*", for they are continuously patient and kind. Much success to each of you!

My desire for the reader is to have friends like the women listed on this page.

Introduction

The Women of AngelFire return to the Inn for another annual retreat, but this year has a few more "firsts". Each of the women was given a golden opportunity in the first story of the series, and now we discover what each has accomplished. The year brought choices – and the repercussions of choices - In love, career, and family. Even a few men join us this year!

Caroline's late husband Frank, still lingers at the Inn, but this time he is not alone. More is revealed about Frank's past and his fortune. Speaking of fortunes, this year we see the varied responses to the newfound prosperity of at least four of our characters.

The young Miss Elaina returns to our story and Reverend Greene is forced to choose between principle, belief and the law.

Marti, now a concert pianist, has the task of building a new career and reconciling the truth about her family. Career building is also the task of Sigrid, our entrepreneurial baker, who unfailingly puts a smile on each page.

All the families of the Women of AngelFire reunite to help Caroline with the one golden opportunity she was unable to give, but promised to give, in the first book of the series.

The Women of AngelFire have a spiritual bond that transcends age, and their ethnic and cultural diversity. For each has accepted the other "*as is*" and simply loved them. Friends are the family we choose and our bonds with them can only open our hearts more fully, more deeply.

The Gathering at AngelFire

Journal Entry: To Frank

Whispers imperceptible
Shadows fractured by a shard of light
A ripple in my vision
I still know when you are near
And no longer have any fear...

Echoes of music in the silence
That fade too quickly
Then like a gentle wave, peace breaks over me

You still want to help me, don't you?
Or protect me?
It's impossible for me to move on, you know
The truth is, I don't really want to
And so...my darling
In veiled love, I wait

Reminiscence

Caroline

C aroline Amoroso sat in the window seat in her third floor residence, overlooking the grand lawns of the AngelFire Inn. She was writing in a journal, but this journal was being used to create plans for the forthcoming annual retreat with her closest friends. This would be the thirteenth year of the annual retreats and would include significant changes from the usual format. *What a year,* she thought; yet as she looked back...the truth was, in the past dozen years, no two gatherings had ever been quite the same. The thirteenth would definitely be extraordinary. The trip to the summit this year would be very different– of that much, she was certain.

Carmen Robles, Caroline's rock-solid, steadfast, assistant manager for the AngelFire Inn, had been diligently planning menus and assisting with arrangements for the events. Her husband, JB, was busily completing a few upgrades on the property and training another horse. In the spring, another foal had arrived, and he and other staff members took great pleasure in caring for it and watching it grow into its spirited personality.

Under the guidance of Robbie Collicci, the newly appointed AngelFire CFO, Caroline, Carmen and JB, carefully planned a few new upgrades for the AngelFire Inn, which included improvements for the interiors of the guest rooms and bungalows. They each held the same vision for AngelFire as its founder, Frank Amoroso, Caroline's late husband. The four of them had worked diligently to regain a number of guests equal to the year before Frank's unfortunate death. Frank had built their clientele through the direct relationship of owners and guests. Caroline had now stepped into that role effortlessly. Their guests seemed appreciative and were happy to share their experiences with their friends, resulting in an increase in business of twenty-three percent over the previous year. They had no desire for celebrity guests and also chose not to advertise in fashionable travel magazines.

Caroline placed the journal on the table next to the window seat along with the four other journals she had filled during the year. Two journals were completed and combined with a photo album that reflected Caroline's experiences in her recent travels with her sister Julia. They had taken the entire month of January to travel the Inca trails to Machu Picchu in Peru. Caroline chose this spiritual center of Peru for her first trip after Frank's death, since this was not a place he would have desired to visit. Caroline, struggling to start a new life without him, wanted to avoid locations that suggested romance or memories of Frank. She and Julia laughed and cried together on this adventure, just as they always had since their youth. Both realized that some of their sisterly traits would never change and that they simply stayed with them, for life. Both understood that acceptance and love were the keys to their lifelong compatibility. It was that same acceptance that kept Caroline's diverse group of women friends harmonious for decades.

One of the two remaining journals held her thoughts, prayers, questions, and yearnings for her late husband Frank. She wrote in it daily. Occasionally, she thought she felt his presence. She would look for him, but regrettably, he no longer appeared to her. Caroline had shared the travel journals with Carmen, but this journal remained private. This journal contained thoughts and feelings from her heart and soul, which still belonged to Frank Amoroso, the love of her life. Not her first love...but indeed her last....or so she thought.

The fifth journal was marked *"Nicole"*. Her first entry was nearly three months ago, and it was slightly overstuffed. It was bulkier and seemed to weigh more than the others. True, it had papers from reports, newspaper articles, additional notes and photos, but the real heaviness of it lay in the emotion connected to the yet unresolved circumstances. Caroline reluctantly picked it up to see if she could make any further sense of what happened. She opened the journal to the very first page where she had documented *the call*. Then, she quickly closed it and placed it back in a bookcase. *Too hard*, she thought, *just too hard*...unable to let it go, she closed her eyes and recalled those painful memories...

Nicole

*"When someone makes an
impression on your soul,
it becomes a 'Heart Print'"*

- Alice Walker

*I*t happened on a Friday evening. Caroline had just finished having a cappuccino with Carmen, while discussing the long day of guests checking out and new guests checking in for the weekend. This changeover often took place within a three hour window, during which the staff rushed to refresh the guestrooms and bungalows. Throughout this transition, JB and Carmen managed the staff, and Caroline processed the incoming and outgoing paperwork.

The telephone rang at about eight-thirty that night. Caroline answered it assuming it was probably a latecomer or a cancellation. It was neither. It was the New Mexico State Police.

"May we speak to Caroline Amoroso?" asked the male voice

"This is she. Who is calling please?" she returned.

"Ma'am, this is Officer Angulo from the State Police. Your name and number are on the cell phone of a Ms. Nicole Roberts, as an I.C.E. call. I am calling you from the Santa Fe area," he said.

"I.C.E. call? That means this is an *emergency* – Oh my God! – What's happened to her? Is she all right? Is Paula with her?" blurted Caroline. Carmen stood and leaned in to hear the conversation.

"There's been an accident," said the officer. "Ms. Roberts is being transported to St. Vincent's Regional Medical Center. Do you know where that is?"

"Yes... I know it. Can you tell me what happened?"

"Well, Ma'am, we're not exactly sure. But I think you'll need to get to that hospital right away," he answered. "What is your location Ma'am?"

"AngelFire Inn," she answered.

"Then it's best that you come down that mountain carefully, but hurry."

"Have you called Paula?" she asked with her voice cracking.

"You're the only one that answered," he replied.

"St. Vincent's, Ma'am," he said again. "It's best you start out now."

"We'll leave right away," she whispered and hung up. Caroline turned to Carmen. The look on her face told Carmen she was horrified. Carmen called out to JB, who was talking with someone in the dining room. He quickly came into kitchen at the sound of the panic in his wife's voice.

"We need to go to St. Vincent's in Santa Fe," said Caroline.

"I'll get Carmen's car. It will be faster than my truck," answered JB, without even asking who was in trouble. Carmen removed the shawl she was wearing and wrapped it around Caroline's shoulders.

"Call me as soon as you know anything...I'll take care of things here," she said. They heard the car outside the entrance.

As Caroline shot out the front door, she shouted, "Try reaching Paula!" She closed the door behind her. Caroline was headed to Santa Fe, hopefully to rescue and retrieve her former sister-in-law, Nicole. She had almost no information. With fear in her mind and prayer in her heart, she and JB descended the mountain toward Taos, en route to Santa Fe.

Carmen called Paula and Nicole's home in Placitas, only to hear their voicemail greeting. She tried to leave a message that conveyed a sense of urgency, yet without panic. She also tried Paula's cell phone, which went straight to voicemail, indicating that it had been turned off. In about a half an hour, she tried both phones again with the same results. Carmen decided to go to her office and get online to find contact information on Paula's place of employment. The Albuquerque Youth Orchestra did not perform during the summer, although there were a number of music camps and workshops that Paula could be attending with her young musicians. Carmen could not find a single scheduled event for that night. She continued to call both numbers every twenty minutes until she would finally reach Paula.

Nicole and Paula led incredibly busy lives. Paula had achieved her dream of becoming the conductor of a youth orchestra program that was organized, well-funded, and outside the public school system. The challenges of her position with the orchestra were the demands on her time and the toll it was beginning to take on her fragile health. Nicole had taken a position as an advanced math teacher, at a charter high school in Santa Fe. She was in the midst of living her dream of creating a multi-media math and science motivational program, encouraging children and teens to focus on the future of their education, particularly in the fields of math and the technology sciences. Nicole was dedicated to her students and committed to this program and it allowed her creativity to soar.

St. Vincent's Hospital was normally a full two hour drive from AngelFire. Caroline and JB barely spoke. She fought to keep herself from falling into the trap of thinking the worst. JB was keenly focused on the road and drove much faster than usual. She thought he might be praying too, or whispering a Zuni chant, as he seemed to be mouthing something inaudible. Again Caroline tried to reach Paula – without success. Then, she decided to call her son, Jarrod in Los Angeles. Hey mom, what's up?" he said answering the phone. For a brief moment Caroline wondered when her nearly-thirty year old son was going to start speaking like an adult. She decided to waste no time and said "Jarrod, please call your father and give him my number. I need to speak to him right away."

"He's here with us right now. We just had dinner. I'll go get him."

In a moment, the familiar voice of her ex-husband Ric Roberts, responded to her call, "Hello Caroline, how are you?" said Ric, warmly.

"Ric, its Nicole – she's been in an accident. She's at St. Vincent's in Santa Fe. Can you come right away? I think this is serious."

"As soon as possible, St. Vincent's – Thanks for the call," he said, and hung up. He was not usually a man who expressed himself with such verbal economy.

"This should be interesting," Caroline said to JB. "I haven't seen my ex-husband in years." Her thoughts went to their last meeting, which had been awkward. It was her son Jarrod's graduation from UCLA, the Alma Mater of his parents, and grandparents. Ric had accompanied his mother and Nicole. Caroline had attended the graduation with Julia, while Frank stayed behind to manage the Inn. Seeing each other brought on a flood of old memories that warmed their hearts. "You will like him, JB. He's usually a very congenial man," said Caroline, as she brought herself back to the present.

"You're not joking, are you?" asked JB.

"No, I'm not. Nicole is his sister. If she's in serious trouble, he needs to be here."

JB kept focused on the highway, and at last, brought Caroline to the emergency entrance to St. Vincent's Medical Center at approximately ten o'clock. He left Caroline at the door and went to park the car.

Caroline went to the ER triage reception and asked about Nicole. She was told that Nicole had been transferred to the Intensive Care Unit. Caroline found her way to the unit, but before she entered, she turned and saw JB coming up the hall toward her. She waited for him and together they entered the unit. A uniformed security guard stopped them, took their names, and escorted them to the nurse's station. A male nurse in blue scrubs gave them Nicole's room number. About twelve feet away behind a sliding glass door, in a small cubicle of a room, Nicole lay unconscious, on a respirator. She was surrounded, injected and plied with I.V.'s, tubes, and monitors. Her face was swollen and bruised. Lacerations on her upper arms bled through the gauze that wrapped them, and more bandages were wrapped around her head.

Caroline gasped at the sight of her. She went to Nicole's side, took her hand, and softly said, "Niki, it's Caroline. I know you can hear me. We're here now, and everything is going to be all right." There was no response. The only sounds were the beep of the monitor and the haunting rhythm of the ventilator. Nicole was not able to breathe on her own.

After a moment of silence, JB said, "I'd like to find a police officer who may be able to tell us something. Will you be okay?"

"I'll be fine; please see what you can find out," she answered.

JB stopped at the nurse's station and asked if an officer had been waiting there for them. "There was one waiting outside the unit," said one of the nurses. "Maybe he went for coffee. The cafeteria is downstairs." JB found the elevators and just as he was ready to board one going to the lower level, he noticed an officer coming out of another.

"Sir – Officer? Can I speak with you for a moment?" asked JB.

"I'm on my way to the I.C.U., if you want to walk with me," he answered.

"Are you officer Angulo?" JB asked.

"Yes, I am. Are you here for the Roberts woman?" he asked.

"Yes, can you tell me what happened?"

"Well it's hard to tell...there will have to be an investigation," said the officer. "Are you a relative?"

"No sir. I am here with Ms. Robert's sister-in-law Caroline Amoroso, who is with her now." The two men made their way back to the Intensive Care Unit. JB went in and got Caroline so she could hear a report on the accident. Introductions were made and they looked for a private place to talk.

The three sat together in a nearby consultation room. "You made awfully good time from AngelFire," said Angulo. Neither JB nor Caroline responded. "So here's what we know...there was an OnStar call to the 911 call center at about eight o'clock. My partner and I got a call from the call center, giving us the location. When we drove up, the ambulance had already arrived. Her car was wrecked...I'd say it was totaled. The paramedics removed her from the car and brought her here. Then I called you."

"What about the other car? Was anyone else hurt?" asked JB.

"There was no other car...at the scene anyway," he answered. "There's no light out there now to see what happened; we'll know more in the morning. It looked like her car rolled over a couple of times. It could have been that she somehow lost control of the car and rolled it herself."

JB and Caroline exchanged glances. "Thank you, Officer Angulo," said JB. "I expect you will know more in the morning.

Caroline added, "In the meantime, I want to get back to her, and we have more calls to make." JB and Officer Angulo shook hands and promises were made to relay more information in the morning. JB called Carmen, while Caroline returned to Nicole's bedside.

By eleven o'clock, JB and Caroline were having coffee in a waiting area outside the I.C.U.

"I can't tell the extent of her injuries, or if she is in a drug induced coma. The nurse is keeping such a close watch and keeps telling me the attending physician will be here shortly to bring us up to date. I haven't been able to grab her chart and read it yet," said Caroline. "They are either being purposefully vague, or they really don't know very much.

I knew several people at this hospital a dozen years ago, so if I'm lucky and find a familiar face, I'll try to get more information from them. Have you spoken with Carmen?"

"Yes, and she's running out of ideas as to how to reach Paula. We'll just have to wait; she will find her. My wife's the daughter of a tracker...it will come to her, one way or another. She always has a way of knowing exactly where I am, that's for sure." It was the first moment either of them had smiled in hours. By eleven-fifteen, Caroline returned to Nicole's bedside. She spoke softly, gently stroked her face, and prayed.

At eleven-thirty, Ric Roberts walked into the room. He was shocked at the sight of his sister. He gave Caroline a quick hug and then took her place at the bedside. He picked up his sister's limp hand and said, "Niki, honey, its Ric. We're going to get you out of here as soon as possible and take you home where you can recover more comfortably. You're going to be okay." He looked over toward Caroline; his tears mirrored hers. He motioned to Caroline to step out of the room with him so that he could find out what happened. Caroline took him outside the unit to talk.

"First, I want you to meet JB Robles. JB, this is Ric Roberts, Nicole's brother, and my ex-husband." The men cordially shook hands.

"So what exactly happened?" asked Ric.

"No one seems to know very much yet," Caroline answered. "I got a call at eight-thirty from a state policeman, who said that there had been an accident, and that Niki was in an ambulance on her way to this hospital.

"The officer said they would look at the scene in the morning, when they had enough light to try and figure out what happened," said JB.

Caroline looked at JB and said, "Since Ric is here, and we don't know how long I'll be here, you should probably go back to AngelFire. Are you okay to drive back up there tonight or would you like to stay in a hotel?"

"I have had enough coffee tonight to drive to New York," answered JB. "I'll be okay." He rose, shook hands with Ric, and embraced Caroline. "Call us in the morning," he said, then, he walked out of the hospital.

Caroline turned to Ric and said, "If you will go to Niki, I'll go over to the ER and see if I can find anyone I know. Maybe I can get some more information." She went back to the ER and walked directly to the triage desk. A young nurse, barely out of school, gave her the names of two nurses and a resident who had cared for Nicole. Caroline did not recognize any of the names. She left the reception area and waited outside in the hall until a pair of electric doors opened as a patient was taken out by gurney toward the surgery department. Caroline slipped in the backside of the emergency rooms and headed for the nurses station, hoping to find a familiar face. She pulled a notebook and pen out of her purse. One of the two nurses she was looking for came forward. Caroline introduced herself as a social worker and said she was looking for information on Nicole Roberts. Was she present when the ambulance arrived? Did she know the EMTs? Which service? Was Nicole conscious when she arrived? Did she say anything? What treatment did they provide? Could she look at the documentation? The nurse was cooperative and although she answered Caroline's questions, there were few details as to what had happened.

As Caroline was heading back to the I.C.U., her cell phone rang. It was Carmen. She had finally reached Paula at eleven o'clock. Paula had been at a fundraising dinner for the Youth Symphony and Orchestra Programs and was now on her way to the hospital. By Caroline's calculations, she should be arriving any moment. Caroline hurried back to the unit.

"Sorry Ma'am you will have to wait," said the security officer, as he stopped Caroline at the entrance to the unit. "Three people would be too many."

Caroline saw Paula, leaning over Nicole and talking. From across the room, Caroline could see the agony on her face. She knew the feeling...all too well. As hard as she was trying not to, Paula was falling apart.

Within minutes, Ric came out of the unit, looking for Caroline.

"Well, *that* was awkward," he said. "I didn't know who this Paula person was. She came in the room and started to cry and all I manage to say was *'who are you?'* This is the woman Niki bought the house with – right? She's a musician or something – right? Even more surprising is her uncanny resemblance to Niki."

"Where have you been the past year, Ric? Paula is Nicole's *partner*. They've been together for almost two years. I know your mother knows about this and so do Brad and Jarrod."

"Oh......Obviously, I don't remember any discussion about this, Caroline. I don't purposefully make a fool out of myself. So she's Niki's *partner?* My sister has decided she is gay? Or is this another one of my sister's *projects?* Sorry, I guess we can talk about that later. Were you able to get any information?"

"I spoke to the ER nurse who took care of her. Niki was unconscious when she arrived. I will need to talk to the EMTs and we'll need to see if the OnStar people have any information. The state police officer knew nothing. We should get more from them in the morning."

"Look, this is going to be a long night. Let me take over the investigation. I'll call Richardson in the morning and speed this up. You go back and take care of Paula and Niki," said Ric.

"You know our governor?"

"Of course I do," answered Ric. This was the Ric Roberts that was about to get in gear, pull strings, and get to the bottom of this whole disaster.

Caroline returned to Paula and Nicole. When she entered the room, Caroline embraced Paula, who then broke down and sobbed. Nicole did not respond in any way. Caroline dug deep into the courage she held within, as they held a vigil all through the night.

By morning, Ric took them to the private conference area and announced his findings – in between his other calls. He was on his cell phone handling business, family calls, and the investigation, all at once, just as he always did. Caroline and Paula sat attentively and endured his distractions.

And Ric began... "The Santa Fe police are now involved, and the state police have determined that this was a *hit and run* incident. There is a long blue streak on one side of Nicole's white Prius. From the height of it, they suspect a pickup truck. The EMT said she was in and out of consciousness twice and only called for Paula. He didn't think she could feel any pain. She did try speaking to the OnStar people, but it was hard for them to hear or understand her. Their recording is garbled with screams, other voices, and they think Nicole said *"my kids"* or something like that. She also yelled out to a "Paul", who I am assuming they meant was Paula. They are sending me a copy of their recording. I should have it tomorrow."

Ric offered to stay at the hospital, while Caroline and Paula went to the house in Placitas to shower and change clothing.

While Paula was showering, Caroline called Carmen and relayed the news. Carmen's unwavering support for both of them came right through the phone. Since Frank's death, Carmen and JB had become her stalwarts.

"JB and I will be strong for you, Caroline, and we will take care of everything. Right now, you need to go outside of yourself and be strong for Paula. I don't think she has anyone else."

Paula and Caroline returned to the hospital. Both wanted to delve further into Ric's report, but before their conversation began, they were approached by a doctor. He was about to go off duty, and wanted to speak with them. The doctor introduced himself as Dr. Hillerman and joined them in the same consultation room officer Angulo had used about ten hours before.

"I wish I had some good news for you," said Dr. Hillerman. "Ms. Roberts has had a serious head trauma. She is not breathing on her own and, well, we will have to give her another day or two to see if she regains consciousness," he said. "We think she slipped into the coma before she arrived here at St. Vincent's, but don't know that for sure. Let's see what happens in the next forty-eight hours.

I know this may sound premature, but her driver's license is in her chart and it indicates that she is an organ donor. So I will have to put in a call about that. Now, no one will contact you, unless it becomes apparent that she is not going to make it."

"Wait, are you saying that she's dying?" said Paula, collapsing backwards into her chair.

"The prognosis is not good, so I am obligated to tell you this. I'm sorry. I know this is hard," said Dr. Hillerman. The doctor rose from his chair and quietly left the three stunned family members in the room.

Ric was the first to speak. "It's not over," he said – because it was the right thing to say.

A week later, the same three stunned family members were sitting in a church full of people in Los Angeles, attending the memorial service for Nicole Roberts. Caroline's season of grief had now been extended. People had come in from Chicago, from the school where she and Paula had both taught, and from New Mexico, where she had been employed in Santa Fe, and hundreds of people came from all over California and Washington DC. Many were representatives from various organizations for which Nicole had campaigned, organized, or volunteered.

After the priest gave a traditional service, Ric Roberts gave the eulogy. He opened with, "None of us are ever prepared for an incomprehensible loss such as this. Our family and friends are devastated." He took a moment to compose himself.

"Nicole's life was a more than a mission; it was a "*Calling*" for social responsibility. I don't think I have to read a list of all the organizations my sister Niki was involved with, for I know that each person here today has received innumerable letters over the last two decades, requesting donations for one, if not several, of her many causes. She used to quote an old gospel lyric which had a refrain that said "*One of us in chains – None of us is free*". And a line she often repeated in her fundraising letters was *'We're all in this together —Right?*

Nicole Roberts lived her life with undying dreams and ideals, higher than the laws and teachings of our society. Her mind was like a multi-faceted crystal that knew there was always another way to look at every issue. I will miss her unshakeable faith in the innate goodness of life.

Now, it appears that she has responded to the *"Final call"* and is face to face with our Creator - Probably asking for an explanation!"

Ric invited others who wished to speak to attend the reception at the Roberts home, where their stories would be shared in a less formal atmosphere, knowing some of his sisters antics might not sit well within the walls of the church. Ric continued with gracious words about a life well lived, words which went mostly unheard by Paula. Caroline sat on Paula's left, holding her hand. Brad and Jarrod, her sons, sat to Caroline's left. Mrs. Lila Roberts, Ric and Nicole's mother, sat next to them. Ric had been strong for the boys and especially compassionate with his mother for today, Lila had lost Nicole, her baby girl.

Behind the Roberts family sat Marti, Kate, Diana, and Sigrid. They took turns placing a supportive hand on Paula's or Caroline's shoulders.

Brad Roberts leaned over toward his mother and asked, "Mom, should we be worried about Grandma?"

Caroline whispered, "Look at your dad up there, remember your Aunt Niki, then remember who raised them. She is the strongest one of all."

On the same day, in Santa Fe, another kind of memorial service was being held for Ms. Nicole Roberts. This one was to be held at the high school where Nicole taught advanced math courses. This service was for her students and the parents who had worked with her on special projects. It was closed to the public. Grief counselors were present to help students grieve the loss of their beloved teacher.

Carly Simmons was one of the parents who was scheduled to speak, and who would also be available to assist grieving students. Her talk was prepared, and she was dressed and ready to leave for the service. Her sixteen year old daughter, Cheri, seemed to be dragging her feet.

"Come on Cheri, we can *not* be late for this today," she yelled down the hall toward her daughter's room.

There was no response from the room. No *"I'm coming – I'm coming!"* shouted back at her.

Carly waited another three or four minutes, and then headed down the hall in a fury. She pounded on her daughter's door and said, "I know this is hard, but we are not going to be late for this service. And *yes* you have to go...Cheri? Do you hear me?"

Again there was no answer. Carly knocked first – then walked directly in Cheri's room. She was sitting on the floor, gazing forward. Her eyes were red from crying, apparently all night.

Cheri spoke, without looking at her mother. "Mom...I have something I have to tell you. I can't keep this secret anymore. It's going to kill me."

Carly remained standing, crossed arms over her chest and leaned against the bedroom door.

Her daughter spoke in an eerie, monotone voice. "Mom...I was there when Ms. Roberts died. I told you that I was going to a sleep-over at Marianna's. It is where I spent the night... but we did not sleep that night. We went out partying with some boys... It just got out of hand. We were out on a country road, just past Pecos, drinking some beer. I didn't think we could hurt anyone out there... There were four of us in the pick-up truck. It was his dad's and we were getting pretty drunk......I guess we were swerving on the road..." She stopped to wipe her eyes, then continued, "Anyway, Ms. Roberts saw us. She drove up behind us and was honking her horn and trying to get us to stop. She pulled up alongside us, rolled down her windows and kept yelling,

"Pull over! Pull over!" The music was loud; we were drunk and Marianna's boyfriend pulled a shotgun off the gun rack and pointed it at her. It wasn't loaded, I swear...By then Marianna and I were screaming. It all happened so fast...," she said. She began sobbing while she continued her story. "We were all screaming about the gun, and the other boy was trying to drive and pull the gun away at the same time. He swerved and we sideswiped Ms. Roberts' car, front to back. She was screaming now, too. I don't think I will ever forget the look on her face. She jerked the car away from the truck, and her car flipped over and over, and then rolled to a stop. When we finally stopped the truck, Marianna and I ran toward her car....The boys didn't come with us. When we saw her, we thought she was already dead... We watched for a minute to see if she would wake up or something, but she didn't... I'm sorry, Mom...We killed her."

Carly Simmons dropped to her knees... "Who was the boy... the driver...who?"

"His name is Paul...Paul Davies."

Love in the Bakery

"Nothin' says lovin' like something from the oven"

- Pillsbury Doughboy

Carmen had just finished a brief staff meeting, delegating assignments for the day, when the phone rang. It was Siggy, who now identified herself as Sigrid Kerrington. Her circumstances had drastically changed since she opened the commercial bakery last year. Sigrid was a creative, industrious woman who was fortunate enough to own a business she loved. Her bakery, officially named Sigrid's Symphony Sweets, produced and sold her elegant mini-*'two-bite pies'* to restaurants from Santa Barbara to San Diego.

"Sigrid! It's so nice to hear your voice," said Carmen. "I've been tracking your progress through your emails and website – It sounds like you are having a wonderful year. Caroline and Robbie are both convinced you will surpass your goals this year."

"I could not have done this without them. Robbie Collicci is brilliant, Carmen. If Kate ever decides not to marry him, I might have to marry him myself," said Sigrid. "So is Caroline nearby? I have to ask her a question. And please give that *hunk-a-hunk-a* man of yours a hug for me."

"Will do," answered Carmen with a hearty laugh. She called out to Caroline and found her coming in from the barn after a morning ride. "Ms. Sigrid Kerrington is on the phone, asking for you. She's certainly seems happy!" she said, handing over the phone.

"Good morning Siggy, how are you?" asked Caroline, as she poured herself a cup of coffee and slid into the booth in the breakfast nook. "Thanks for sending the pumpkin cream pies. We'll definitely be ordering those for the rest of the year, although you have caused a new form of discipline around here that we like to call the *"Keep Your Hands Off The Pies Diet"*.

"Well that's certainly not the case here – I've lost another dress size since our last meeting," responded Sigrid. "Caroline...Marti called this morning, and she said that you're considering moving our annual retreat to the last week in September, rather than the end of August. I am calling to let you know that I would actually prefer coming in the autumn this year, for several reasons. Aspens in autumn are gorgeous, and then I will have completed my third quarter sales for the bakery, too. I can meet with you and Robbie, at AngelFire. *And* I have a request...Oh, excuse me someone just knocked on my office door."

Caroline heard Sigrid answer the door, speak with someone, then cross the room singing *"Love is in the Air,"* the old theme song from *"The Love Boat"*. She smiled and winked at Carmen, covered the mouthpiece and whispered, "Sounds like there's love in the bakery."

Sigrid returned to the phone, and said "Now where was I? What was I saying, Caroline? Oh, yes, the retreat... Remember last year, that JB, Robbie and Jackson attended at our farewell dinner? Well, I would like to invite someone and introduce him to the group at this year's celebration. Would that be okay?"

"Why Sigrid Kerrington...what have you been up to?" said Caroline. "Do you have something you want to share?"

"I might as well tell you, it's Arturo Montecito, our Master Baker. He's been such a great help to me, and we really do enjoy each other's company," answered Siggy.

"Of course you can bring him. Especially this year...," said Caroline. "I have to tell you that in June, while on the airplane, returning from our last meeting with you, Robbie said he suspected that you two were an item. I guess he was right!"

"Well," said Siggy. "Nearly everything in my life is going beautifully right now. I have a successful business, my health is good, I'm losing weight, ...and let's face it Caroline...*When you're HOT – You're HOT!*"

Sigrid's Year

The success of Sigrid Kerrington's bakery was as much of a delight to her friends as it was to Sigrid. Robbie, on behalf of Caroline, had handled the purchase of the vacant Pattie's Pies building, which in turn, was refurbished and leased back to Sigrid's newly formed corporation for a nominal amount. Robbie and Sigrid's attorney drew up a contract whereby Caroline and Robbie stayed on her governing board, with an agreement that if or when Sigrid's business could afford to buy the building, it would become hers at the original purchase price. Robbie and Caroline met with Sigrid, quarterly. Their intentions were to support her and keep their guidance minimal. She surprised both of them with her business acumen. Caroline soon discovered that Sigrid, consistently, had thoroughly researched her options before each decision was made.

Sigrid was determined to make this operation successful. She wanted that *Sara Lee status* of her dreams. This meant long hours, eating on the run, and huge responsibilities. It also meant physical exhaustion. She was losing weight, looking good, but not always feeling great. That is, until one early morning about four a.m., when her master baker, Arturo came into the bakery to begin his day and found Sigrid in her office with her head on a hot pink satin pillow, on her desk. Sigrid had worked late and fallen asleep in her office. He woke her with a cup of coffee and an offer to take her home. She was grateful – very grateful. He had his assistant take over and, as he drove her home, Arturo praised her for her dedication and warned her of her over-compensating for her well hidden insecurities. He tenderly escorted her to her door, kissed her on the forehead, and insisted she take the day off and rest.

Sigrid trusted him and found his tenderness incredibly appealing. She was also confused.

Arturo was an employee in a key position. She had to protect her vulnerability as a woman, as well as protect her business. For two weeks she merely smiled at him and kept to business as usual.

Perhaps she smiled a little brighter, or there was something in their eye contact that encouraged him. For one day, at the end of the workday he came into her office to talk. He closed the door behind him and sat down squarely in front of her. And then he smiled...a sweet, admiring smile.

"I want to thank you," he said.

"For what?" responded Sigrid.

"For being so respectful; for making this a place of laughter, which makes it a pleasure to work here; for making all the employees feel that they are part of something big; for being shrewd and not a shrew. Do you know how unusual this is?" offered Arturo.

"Why...no...I'm used to working with children. I hoped it wouldn't show too much," she answered.

"Well it does... a little," he confessed.

"It does? How?"

"Are you aware of the fact that you call Pamela – Pammy? And Robert – Bobbie? And Jose – Jo-Jo? And..."

"Okay, I get it. Have I done that with everyone?" she asked, while rolling her eyes.

"No...you don't do it to me. I am still Arturo to you," he started.

But before he could say another word, Siggy blurted, "But you're a man!"

"I am, and awfully glad you see me that way. And because of that, I would like to ask you to go out for an early dinner today, after work," he asked, with a gentle smile.

"Why?" said Siggy, now a bit befuddled.

"Because you are a woman – a fine woman," he answered. "And Ms. Sigrid, my friends call me Artie."

And that was in the spring. By summer, he was Artie, and as autumn was now approaching, a few "Honeys" and "Dears" and "Sweeties" slipped in, and the relationship was beginning to bloom and seemed quite promising.

Adagio for Heartstrings

A crisp September morn...
Under pure azure skies
Mother Nature's paint box
Splashed gloriously, before our eyes
A salutation so divine
For the gathering of good friends

Caroline and Carmen had breakfast together to review last minute details for the retreat. Both women were anticipating fun-loving times and peaceful, inspirational moments. They were also hopeful that they would uplift the sorrows of those who had suffered losses in the past year.

Carmen offered to go to the airport with Caroline to pick up Marti, but Caroline declined. Marti and Caroline's friendship was deeply-rooted in the secrets of Marti's past. Revealing those secrets had caused much turmoil with those she loved. Caroline was hoping to have the few hours of travel to convey her unceasing support and encouragement for her weary friend.

Marti's saving grace was her burgeoning career as a composer and concert pianist. Winning the Pacific Symphony's competition last year had opened many doors for her. Caroline was optimistic, that in time, Marti's life would become truly happy again.

The freeways were especially crowded with caravans of motor homes and campers. Caroline suspected these were early-bird travelers or participants in the upcoming International Balloon Fiesta. All camps and RV parks would be booked solid for the next month due to the uniqueness of this event. Balloonists from all over the world came to Albuquerque to compete in the spectacular festivities. Caroline had wanted to plan a day at the Fiesta for her friends, but when Carmen started trying to make certain reservations for the group, they realized they had waited too long. Too much had happened and somehow the time had slipped by.

The airport also turned out to be busier than usual. Caroline found Marti looking tired and drawn, at the baggage claim area. They had just seen each other a few months earlier when she and Robbie had their quarterly meeting with Sigrid, and Caroline was concerned about her then. The stress of the past year had taken its toll on her.

Warm greetings and prolonged hugs and the promise of lunch at a great restaurant lifted Marti's spirits, a little. Caroline gave Marti three restaurant options and she chose The Corn Maiden, at the Tamaya Resort at the Santa Ana Pueblo.

"You look good," said Marti. "Not that *widow-thin* look you had last year. You must be feeling well, too. I see a little blush on those cheeks. Have you been spending more time riding?"

"And you must have spoken with Dr. Kate, since you are checking out my coloring," responded Caroline. "You probably know she's already here in New Mexico. She's at Robbie's place in Santa Fe. They'll be driving up to AngelFire tomorrow. She spends as much time with him as her schedule allows. I was almost afraid she wasn't going to join us this year. You – Martha Westerlund – on the other hand, look like you need a good rest.

This week away from L.A. should do wonders for you. I have planned a little pampering this week. I think we all need it."

"Sounds like *you've* been talking to Dr. Kate," said Marti. "I'm fine – I just need a good night's sleep. Maybe Dr. Woo-Woo will work up some of her famous knock-out drops for me this year."

They kept the conversation light as they drove the long road into the Santa Ana Pueblo and arrived at the Tamaya Resort & Spa with its classic adobe architecture and glorious views of the Sandia Mountains. They strolled leisurely through the lobby and were awed by the splendid art collection. The rear walls of the main building were an expanse of glass which incorporated the views of the river and golf course, cradled by the mesas and the mountains.

The Corn Maiden restaurant had an open exhibition kitchen where one could observe the culinary talents of the chef. Marti ordered the jicama wrapped lobster ravioli and Caroline ordered the sweet potato and apple soup and a salad. While they waited for their food to arrive, they enjoyed a glass of wine from one of the local vineyards.

"Tell me Marti, are you physically tired, or are you just weary over the rift between you and Erik?"

"Erik Jr. or Erik Sr.? Which rift are you referring to?" answered Marti.

"And this too...shall pass," said Caroline. "Your son is just confused; he'll come around. I know Erik; he loves you dearly. And as for his father...well, that one will play itself out, too. I bet you stirred up emotions in him that he never knew still existed. When we went to Sweden, I saw the look on his face. You've opened up a part of his heart he had closed off a long time ago."

"I knew this wouldn't be easy, but I've never experienced my son's anger like this before. I want this to be settled soon. I miss laughing with him, and I have two granddaughters, for heaven's sake. One of them asked me why her daddy was so mad all the time. I know that Erik will come around. I just hope he comes *all* the way around...back to the way things were."

Do you really think that is possible? Caroline thought. "This may take more time, but I think his Aunts' Caroline, Katie and Siggy will step in, if this doesn't clear up soon. Actually, since we will all be together this week, maybe we can figure out a way to make that happen. How did Laney handle the news? I didn't get much time with her at the concert."

"Laney is a rock," answered Marti. She's so busy with her little ones that she doesn't give it much energy. She has been an ally, really. She doesn't condone or judge my actions. We're all at the acceptance stage – walking on eggs, and keeping our conversations polite."

"Well, that's good news – very good news. It can only get better from there."

"From your lips to God's ears...." said Marti, while rolling her eyes.

"I do keep you in my prayers, you know," said Caroline. "Well my dear, this is the first meal of the 13th Annual AngelFire Retreat," said Caroline, as she raised her glass. "Here's to a fine company of friends."

Marti's Year

*M*arti's year was one of professional advancement and one that included a major setback in her personal life. Doors were opening and doors were not quite closing, but a few were slammed in the heat of the moment.

After what had seemed a lifetime as a church organist and piano teacher, Marti's composition for the Pacific Symphony won a grand prize award, and she was becoming the concert pianist she had dreamed of, with bookings all over the state. Almost simultaneously, she had revealed the truth to her son about his father, and to his father, the truth about a son. Both were outraged at her for having kept their identities secret for decades.

Victory – Defeat – Pleasure – Pain; *was life ever just all good? -* Marti wondered.

Marti and her first love, Erik, were reunited in Sweden, with Caroline along for moral support. It was the first time either had laid eyes on the other since that pivotal summer in their college days - the summer of love for two young, starry-eyed college students. A blond-haired, blue-eyed Swedish foreign exchange student and an African-American music major, from Michigan – their future together was doomed from the outset. Marti's fundamentalist parents forbade the relationship, and to complicate matters further, Marti soon discovered she was going to have a child – Erik's child. Erik returned to his homeland heartbroken and unaware of his pending fatherhood.

Their reunion was bittersweet, for so many years had gone by, they barely recognized each other. Not until they were eye to eye, did they see the lover of their youth. There were awkward silences, and moments into which, thankfully, Caroline interjected her lighthearted humor. Both were reticent to ask too many questions.

Seeing Erik in Sweden was almost more than she could handle. Rushes of old memories, regrets of promises not kept, and the rejection of her parents, made sleep nearly impossible. She and Caroline were in disagreement over telling Erik that he had a son. Marti insisted she would wait for the right moment – but that *moment* didn't come.

While Erik was delighted to see Marti, he was deeply entrenched in mourning, for he had recently lost his wife of twenty-six years, to leukemia. He spoke of her often, as well as of his son William, who was about to graduate from college.

While Caroline was disappointed in the absence of full disclosure, she understood that time would take care of this. She didn't believe it was an accident that Erik had found her, but perhaps a little *Divine Intervention*, so that Marti could bring forth the truth to her son.

And the truth did come forward...but certainly not in the way anyone had hoped.

Initially, Erik had found Marti on the Internet. He was scheduled to attend an architect's conference on green technology in Los Angeles. While perusing entertainment options, he noted a Martha Westerlund as one of four finalists in a competition for the Pacific Symphony. He wondered if this could possibly be the same Martha Westerlund from his days as a foreign exchange student in his junior year of college. He contacted the symphony offices and found a sympathetic ear, who took his email address and forwarded it to Marti. She held on to it for weeks before responding. This was dangerous territory for her. She had made a choice, created a life with her son, and left Erik out of the picture. Then, it seemed that life interfered on its own. She had to make a new choice, and with the help of her friend Caroline, she responded.

⸙

It was late September, and was the annual awards night for the New Composers Competition for the Pacific Symphony, held at Segerstrom Concert Hall, at the Orange County Performing Arts Center. It was a grand evening and in attendance to support Marti, were Caroline and her sister Julia, Paula and Nicole, Sigrid and Kate, along with Marti's son, Erik and his wife, Laney. Marti had arranged for Erik and Laney to have fourth row seats, while the others sat several rows behind them.

Caroline observed that the four finalists were of mixed ages and ethnicity, reflecting another gift of the arts.

Julia noticed that there appeared to be as many women in the orchestra as men, with quite a wide age range, which also was gratifying to see. "God bless the Arts in America" she whispered to Caroline.

The orchestra played an opening concerto, and then the conductor discussed the special performers of the evening. He praised the versatility of their work and assured the audience of how difficult it would be to choose this year's winner.

Soon after, they brought out the first of the four finalists. He was a twenty-five-year-old pianist born in Thailand. The young man clearly felt every note of his composition. It was a pleasure for the audience to watch his physical expressiveness. When the applause subsided, he thanked his adoptive parents for his education and their support. His music and performance were breathtaking.

The second finalist was a thirty-something, fiery redheaded, single mother, originally from Maine. She stated that she had been playing piano since the age of five and started composing at the age of ten. Her composition was as fiery as her hair and as stormy as a winter in Maine. It evoked resounding applause.

The intermission offered the opportunity for a glass of wine for the party of five, and a pleasant visit for Erik and his Aunts. Each of them was eager to hear Marti's composition, and each was surprised to know it would be Erik's first time to hear it as well. Erik and Laney decided to see if they could find Marti and give her a few last words of encouragement. He was so very proud of his mother, regardless of whether or not she won the competition. So they left the lobby to see if they could get backstage.

Just before the chimes called for everyone to return to their seats, Kate and Sigrid noticed that the line to the ladies room had finally dwindled, so they dashed off. Paula and Nicole headed back toward the concert hall to return to their seats.

Caroline and Julia lingered near the bar, deciding whether to split one of the sweets displayed before them, when out of the corner of her eye, Caroline saw him. It was Erik – not junior, but senior. She grabbed Julia's arm as he came toward them.

Julia tried hard not to let her jaw drop open as Caroline whispered who was approaching. "Erik! How nice to see you. What a surprise!" said Caroline. "May I introduce you to my sister Julia?"

Julia, known for her quick wit, only managed to say, "How lovely to finally meet you. Does Marti know you are here?"

"No, actually, she doesn't," he answered. "I just arrived and I had to buy a ticket outside from someone whose relative was unable to make it. Apparently this event was sold out. I'm actually staying in Los Angeles for a conference."

"Life's an adventure isn't it?" said Julia, anticipating the now unpredictable outcome of the night.

"Do you have a program?" asked Caroline. The moment those words came out of her mouth, she wanted to take them back for she had just handed him the title of Marti's composition. "Where are you sitting?" she said, hoping to distract him from reading the program.

"Let's see...I am in row 10, seat 134," he answered.

"Wonderful, we're just two rows behind you," said Julia. "Almost directly behind you..."

And six rows behind your son...thought Caroline. The sounding chimes indicated that they must return to their seats. So with the exchange of a few pleasantries, they walked back into the music hall together.

The third finalist was a man in his mid-fifties, from Salt Lake City. During the conductor's introduction, he waved to his wife and nine children sitting in the second row. He remarked that with his large family, he and his wife both had well-earned white hair. His composition was strong and determined, with religious undertones, reflecting his rock solid faith.

By this time, Paula had declared by whisper, that the first finalist was Marti's strongest competitor. The young man's vigorous finger movements and intriguing melodic passages would be difficult to surpass.

Then came the moment Marti's family and circle of friends were waiting for. After a heartfelt introduction, Martha Westerlund, the most senior finalist came forward on the stage and shook the hand of the conductor. Caroline and Julia squeezed each other's hands.

"All compositions tell a wonderful story and most have a great back story," said the maestro. "Ms. Westerlund...would you like to tell us yours?"

"I think I would prefer that the music speak for itself. It is a very personal story about my life," she answered.

"Ladies and gentleman, I give you Ms. Martha Westerlund, our fourth finalist, with her composition entitled 'Erik's Theme'".

Erik Sr. turned to look at Caroline quizzically. She did not respond, for there were no words to say what needed to be said.

The conductor stepped up to the podium, raised his baton and for the next eighteen minutes, Marti's fingers floated across the keyboard, accompanied by thirty-three violins. There were immediate highs and lows with religious overtones, followed by resounding furor. The tender mercies of flutes and woodwinds lifted the spirit of the piece. The violins flowed in with voluptuous passion and romance. Lighthearted moments ensued with the inclusion of French horns, but none escaped the return of the furor. Marti's piece took a bold turn with horns and tympani which marched the audience into the next movement. Silence – 2 – 3 – 4; suddenly sweet, playful sounds which marked the opening of the 2nd movement, which captivated the audience.

Paula was mesmerized, and Nicole noticed that the striking contrasts in Marti's composition kept the audience leaning forward.

Caroline closed her eyes as the music evoked memories of their early years, when she and Marti became friends, the romance with Erik, the furor of Marti's father, and the two of them fleeing to California, baby Erik, college days...it was all flooding back to her. Marti was telling the story of her life. It was a living document of her life's journey. She had reached a place of compassion for herself and this work was a pure expression of love. The music held the warmth and contentment of a deep forest, voiceless, strong and overflowing with beauty.

Tears were in the eyes of Marti's family and friends, as the end of the piece drew near. There was a combination of strings that portrayed a sense of peace which moved into silence...Marti played the last notes and hauntingly stopped as if it were left unfinished...a knowingness that there was more of her story, yet to come.

Erik and Laney were the first to stand for the ovation that waved through the crowd. Paula vigorously applauded and shouted "Bravo!" She didn't have to know the details of Marti's life to understand the story played out in the music.

Julia was astounded and her throat constricted, as she fought back her tears. Kate turned to Caroline and mouthed the word "*magnificent*". Her eyes were just as red and brimming with tears as Caroline's.

Caroline made clear eye contact with Erik Sr. who appeared speechless. He, too, was obviously deeply moved.

As the winners were about to be announced, Caroline's heart pounded, awaiting Marti's jubilant moment. The conductor announced that he would only call out the second and grand prize winners. When the second place award was given to the young man from Thailand, Paula turned to Caroline and whispered – "She won!"

And when the conductor called Marti's name, her family and friends rose to their feet in pure delight. Applause thundered through the concert hall. A crystal award shaped like a treble clef was presented to Martha Westerlund, along with a check for $10,000. Marti wore the brightest, biggest smile her face could give.

When the applause died down, the conductor asked her if she wished to say anything. She spoke a few gracious words of gratitude to the Pacific Symphony, to her music coach and to her friends who had supported her over the years.

"Erik's theme was quite a dramatic composition. Is there an Erik in the audience that we should all acknowledge?" asked the conductor. "Erik, would you please stand...?"

And in that very moment – both Erik Jr. and Erik Sr. stood. Julia leapt up and spoke – "I think all persons named Erik should stand." In total, Sigrid counted eighteen standing Eriks. Erik Sr. started the *"Erik applause"*. Erik Jr. just stood there standing, staring at the man six rows behind him. He was the same height, same body style, same square jaw line and high cheekbones. They locked eyes for only an instant.

Caroline caught that defining moment. She caught the look of mystery in both their faces. She wondered – *did they really know*?

Then both Erik's looked at Caroline.

Julia quickly responded and called out to Erik, Jr., "Go see your mother! This is her big night! Go! Laney, take your husband to his mother! It's her night!

As they turned to move toward the stage, Caroline spoke to Erik Sr., "This is not the right time Erik."

Actually, she had just answered him with all he needed to know. He made his way over to Caroline and said, "Don't tell her I was here. I'll call her tomorrow. I know how much this night means to her. I'm sorry. I have to go back to my hotel and sort this out."

"I'm really sorry about this too, Erik," said Caroline. Erik left without another word.

Julia took her arm, leaned in and said, "Okay now, the last minute didn't happen. You are going to join your friends and celebrate this auspicious occasion. This is just the beginning for Marti. We'll talk about this tomorrow – Tonight we celebrate! "

The Robles' Predicament

"All I ask is the chance to prove that money can't make me happy."

Terence Alan Patrick Seán "Spike" Milligan

*C*aroline and Marti arrived at the AngelFire Inn by mid-afternoon. As they entered the Inn, they heard a door slam. The noise came from the direction of Carmen's office. Caroline called out to Carmen as she rounded the reception desk. Then, she caught a glimpse of JB's back as he swiftly walked toward the kitchen. She started to call out to him, but with a second thought she did not. She turned toward the desk, and she noticed a light on the telephone, which indicated that Carmen was on line two.

Caroline gave Marti the keys to the Annie Oakley Bungalow and said, "Enjoy the new digs! One of the things we did this year was to upgrade the bungalows. I replaced the numbers with a name of a real Cowgirl. I hope you like it! There's a framed description and story of each woman next to her portrait over the fireplace. I really

45

enjoyed the research and it was a great pleasure designing these rooms. I'm afraid it may look a lot like *"Buffalo Bill's Wild West Show goes to Europe"*; because I cannot ignore our architecture... they still had to blend. I just thought it would be fun. "

"Why Cowgirls?" asked Marti.

"I was visiting Robbie and Kate in Santa Fe, and we took a walk down Cannon Road and happened upon a show at an art gallery. I was inspired by a display of paintings of cowgirls. I wanted the whole collection, and the bungalows seemed like the perfect place to put them. I was trying to bring in a little more of the Southwest. We have a good blend in the main areas but not as much in the bungalows. So each painting created a palette for each bungalow. I'm only sorry I had to stop at five," said Caroline.

"It must have been nice to have an unlimited design budget, too," said Marti.

"Well, not exactly unlimited – Robbie created the budget for the decorating, and I was pretty good about sticking to it," answered Caroline. "We're a good team."

"That's what Siggy has said, too. When do you think she will arrive?"

"She is supposed to be here by dinner time...about 7:00 pm, I think," answered Caroline. "I think Diana may also be here by then, and hopefully Paula will too."

"Originally, Siggy was going to fly in with me, but I think she had a hot date," said Marti. "She's been incommunicado for the past two weeks. Must be that she is spending a lot of time with Arturo."

"Did she tell you that Arturo's joining her here on Saturday night?" asked Caroline. "I doubt they've been away; he can't leave the bakery for more than a day at a time right now. There's still so much to do. Remember...our Siggy has big goals."

"That's right – She will be our Twenty-first Century Sara Lee!" said Marti.

"Just pray that she can keep up the work pace! She works very long hours and it's starting to pay off. I just hope that it doesn't tax her health too much. After her bout with altitude sickness last year, I'm happy she's coming up to the mountains at all."

"Okay, I'll head over to meet Miss Annie," started Marti. Before she could finish her sentence, the door opened from Carmen's office and Carmen slowly appeared red-eyed and frowning.

"Carmen, are you okay? What happened?" asked Caroline, putting an arm around her shoulder.

Marti dropped her bags and came to Carmen's side. "Just tell us what happened and who we need to go slap around a little."

"I'm sorry," she answered. "It's really nothing. I just hate it when JB is right about something and has that *'I-told-you-so' attitude*."

"About what?" asked Caroline?

"It's about my car. JB didn't want me to buy a car he couldn't work on and well...I wanted what I wanted. Now I have to take it all the way to Taos for some work, and I'll have to have it towed."

"Ouch! That's got to cost a few pretty silver dollars," said Marti. "That's at least a twenty-five mile ride down the mountain – isn't it?"

"That's one of the problems of living up here," said Caroline. "I have to take my car in to the city, too."

"Well, what kind of car did you buy Carmen, if you don't mind my asking?" said Marti.

"We both bought new cars this year. JB bought a new pick-up truck and I bought a BMW. Against my husband's wishes, I might add. He warned me about this potential problem. You know JB – usually, he can fix anything," said Carmen.

"Except some foreign cars," added Marti. "Is he angry with you for buying the car – because it broke down – or because he can't repair it?"

"All of the above...anyway, I called the tow truck. And I have a dinner to prepare!" said Carmen, drying her eyes, one more time.

"Okay, I'm going to settle in with Miss Annie, and I'll see you later. Let me know if you want me to straighten out your man," Marti quipped.

"And just how do you intend to do that?" asked JB as he entered the foyer.

"Busted! Uh - where did you come from?" returned Marti.

"I thought I heard voices and as soon as I finished my ten count, I decided to come back out and see who was here," said JB. "By the way - Congratulations, I've been hearing some incredible stories about you."

"Thanks, JB," Marti said sincerely.

"Come on, I'll take you over to meet Annie Oakley. Let me take your bags." JB took Marti's luggage and Marti departed singing *"I Can Do Anything You Can Do - Better"* from the play, "Annie Get Your Gun", all the way to the bungalow.

"Oh No You Can't," responded Caroline.

"Oh Yes, I Can...Yes, I Can... YES, I CAN!!" sang Marti, all the way out the door.

Well, she's ready to have a good time tonight, thought Caroline.

Carmen turned to Caroline and said, "If the timing turns out right, Diana and Sigrid are supposed to share a limo ride from Santa Fe and should be here just before dinner. Paula called to send her regrets, but I managed to talk her into coming up tonight instead of tomorrow. Poor girl... she sounded so sad."

"Good work, Carmen. Is there anything I can do to help you with the car situation? I hate to see you and JB upset with each other. It seems to be happening more often lately. Are you sure I can't help with you this?" asked Caroline.

"No Caroline, we'll work it out. We always do," said Carmen. "I want to get the dinner started, okay?"

"Can I ask you one question, and you don't have to answer if you don't want to," said Caroline. "What is the one thing, you and JB argue about the most?"

Without hesitation, Carmen answered, "M-O-N-E-Y." And she turned and walked straight to the kitchen.

"Hmmm..." said Caroline to herself. "I guess Robbie was right."

Carmen & JB's Year

When Caroline first became aware of her financial standings through her husband Frank's estate, her first inclination, after the shock, was to reward Carmen and JB with a generous bonus, for their loyalty and willingness to do whatever it took to keep the business of the AngelFire Inn viable. At the time, there were many unanswered questions regarding Frank's motives for keeping his fortunes hidden. Soon after the revelation, Caroline promoted both Carmen and JB, giving them both a substantial increase in their salaries. The three of them met with Robbie Collicci, who managed the finances of the AngelFire Inn on a regular basis.

JB employed a larger staff, which included more assistance with the grounds and the horses, and the maintenance, construction and security of the all the buildings.

Carmen received administrative and technological assistance from a college student, Marci, who was a marketing major from New Mexico State University, to help improve their advertising plans and events, and to update their technology systems.

Carmen had welcomed the new financial status with enthusiasm, while JB had shown some reluctance and was disinclined to spend much of his new income. Eventually, both of them bought new vehicles. JB bought a new American pick-up truck, and Carmen bought a luxury foreign car. Soon after, Carmen expanded her wardrobe with more designer labels, and had begun to create a jewelry collection of vintage Native American silver, turquoise, and particularly Zuni inlay work. Shopping seemed to bring her great pleasure. JB, on the other hand, did not enjoy shopping at all. Within months, money issues had become a source of contention between them.

Previously, not having money was never an issue for either of them, for they were comfortable and were generously compensated for their work at AngelFire; but for some reason, having even larger amounts of money had called forth deep seated issues that neither of them was comfortable with. *To spend or not to spend....that was a brand new question.*

Carmen felt that over the years they had put off some important purchases and travel, waiting until they could afford them. Now that they were even more financially comfortable – *why not spend the money and enjoy some of the "someday" things they had dreamed of?*

Although, JB loved his new truck, he expected a little more practicality with their newfound income. At first, in his own quiet wisdom, he concluded that Carmen would be the spender, and he would be the saver. It wasn't until Carmen decided to update *his* wardrobe that the fireworks began. Truth be told, they began as sparklers. With a *"How could you pay $200 for those jeans?"* and an *"I'm NOT wearing designer labels on my behind."*

Somehow, that irritated Carmen. *"You've got to get with the times,"* she said or *"You are a handsome man and I want you to look good - head to toe, and inside out."* The real fireworks began when Carmen said, "JB, this is the twenty-first century for Zuni's, too. It's time for you to give up the ponytail."

That was pushing the envelope of patience wide open for JB. He called her a *"Delilah"* inferring that his "Samson" physique required his long hair.

"You've been spending too much time in that Santa Fe Salon," JB told her. "The chemicals in those hair products are making you delusional."

Carmen responded by learning the art of door-slamming.

This was not new territory for the Robles' couple, perhaps just new scenery. Carmen and JB had tackled some major issues in the first four years of their marriage, though the turbulence did settle down as they established their careers –JB in construction, and Carmen in tribal and city administration, and both became more focused on personal career growth. Then, Frank and Caroline offered the couple key roles at AngelFire. The four became a great team, and for the next twelve years, they were secure, peaceful and productive. Working together could have been risky, but instead, thankfully, it deepened their relationship. They became an integral part of another community which had previously been unknown to them.

Frank and JB had known each other briefly – before AngelFire, before Caroline and Frank had married, before success and money became such prevalent issues in their lives. *What happened to us* – wondered JB? *What is it about money that does this to people?*

Carmen had the same questions. She and JB were in new territory in their marriage – a place that should have brought more security, and more pleasure to their lives. She admitted to herself, but not to JB, that she might be looking at their finances as more for pleasure, while his viewpoint was more for security, but there seemed to be something else to this, something deeper within both of them.

The best part of the past year for the Robles' couple, was being a part of the new state-of-the-art high school in Taos. After last summer's fire that destroyed the old high school building, JB, Carmen, parents and Council members, joined forces to rebuild, redesign and create a new compound of buildings to meet the needs of the students and the community.

Caroline remained in the background in order to keep her anonymity as the school's most generous donor. Carmen produced additional community fundraising events, while JB worked with the contractors. Nicole made her contribution by assisting with the design of the new science and technology labs, while Paula aided in the creation of a new music department. Carmen and JB were most proud of the building that was devoted to Native American Studies. A bond measure was passed to raise funds for the continuation of these programs.

It had been another year of satisfying, yet hard work. The school, the improvements made at AngelFire, and the unexpected financial increases, all were due to the legacy of JB's closest friend, Frank Amoroso. On the night that JB and Caroline put the last of the finishing touches on the last bungalow, JB put an arm around Caroline and said "This is really well done, Caroline. You know, I think Frank would have approved."

Caroline put her arm around JB's neck, hugged him and said, "Thank you, JB. I think he would have liked this too."

About fifteen feet away, just outside the bungalow, stood a specter of light, in the shape of a man. He was barely noticeable... he stood there, with a smile... and with both thumbs up.

Dinner is Served

*"Dreams are like stars...you may never touch them,
but if you follow them they will lead you to your destiny."*

efreshed and full of anticipation for an enjoyable dinner with her much loved friends, Marti returned to the dining room at six-thirty. She had awakened from a short nap when she heard a car arrive. Thinking it might be Sigrid, Diana or Kate, she hurriedly prepared for the evening. As Marti arrived in the dining room, she noticed that the wine was iced and the table was set for six, which meant that someone was not going to make it tonight for the first dinner. She went to the kitchen to find Carmen. There were three other very busy people assisting her. One was stirring a pot on the stove, another chopping and slicing, and the third was preparing the plates. Carmen had created something that sent an aroma into the kitchen that made Marti's mouth water. Carmen was intently focused on giving directions to her kitchen staff.

"Hi Carmen, I came over early because thought I would try to help you with dinner, but it looks like you have it all under control," said Marti.

"I do Marti, you see...*we have people for that*, now," said Carmen as she placed finger quotes in the air. "A lot has changed for us this year. I even have an assistant for the office, but Marci has returned to NMSU this month, for a special class. *We have people* for everything"

"Except to fix your foreign car," said Marti.

"Oh – ouch, you're right! I think I'll have to put that on the agenda for our next executive meeting," laughed Carmen.

"Has Caroline come down here yet?" asked Marti.

"Yes, but she was called to the phone. I think she took it in her office, so she is back upstairs. She'll be down soon. Would you like a glass of wine and some hors d'oeuvres?"

"No, I'll wait for the others, thank you. I'll come back at seven," said Marti. She walked back to her cabin, mumbling something that sounded a lot like *"people for that"* and *"my people ... your people...times they are a changing...hmmm."*

At seven o'clock, Marti returned to the dining room and found Caroline pouring a glass of wine for Paula. Both turned to greet Marti with warm smiles and an embrace.

"Don't you look lovely in your ensemble...sage and cream looks gorgeous on you!" said Caroline.

"This is a new color for you isn't it?" asked Paula.

"Yes, I've decided to move out of the black box," said Marti. "Though I'll still wear black on the concert stage."

"I stick to black most of the time, too," said Paula. "It's an unwritten law for concert attire, and one that I may just try to undue one of these days. I'm thinking of having the kids all wear red for a holiday concert or white for another, and well, we'll see what happens. It's also an economic decision for many of my kids."

Caroline silently made a mental note to speak to Paula privately about that idea.

Carmen walked in and greeted everyone with a smile and a sigh of relief. "Dinner will be served as soon as we're all seated. Are we all here now?"

"Katie called and she's decided she would rather make the drive in the morning," said Caroline, withholding the details of their conversation.

"Or...she decided she would rather have one more night with her man," said Marti. "And yes, I *am* both jealous of and happy for her."

"I understand that," said Paula, which brought an awkward, but brief moment of silence.

"Diana and Sigrid haven't arrived yet but should be here any minute. Their itinerary said seven o'clock. I think it would be okay for us to be seated and have a glass of wine and a little appetizer," said Carmen.

"I smell something wonderful," said Paula. "I really have learned to *love* southwestern food!"

"You don't look like you've been eating much of anything," said Carmen. "I was getting concerned, but maybe you will make up for it while you're here."

The four women proceeded to the dining room. When they arrived, the candles had been lit and small trays of vegetable crostini were on the table. A small plate with Carmen's version of Ceviche des Camarones was centered at each place setting. They had each just sampled a first bite when they heard the entry door open. One of the staff was assigned at the entry desk and had been instructed to take the luggage to the appropriate bungalow.

Within a minute or two, Diana entered the room aglow in peach suede pants with a coordinated peach silk blouse. Her hair was pulled back in a sleek chignon. She had just flown across the country and had a nearly three hour ride from the airport and looked as if she were about to step out on the dais.

"Diana Greene! You made it!" said Caroline.

"Welcome!" said Carmen

"It's so wonderful for you to come for this," whispered Paula with a warm hug.

"Are you alone?" asked Marti. "Is Siggy with you?"

"Hi everyone. I'm so grateful the driver made it up the mountain easily, and I'm happy to see you, too" responded Diana, as she worked her way around the table, embracing each of the women.

"Well now, I've just been given the key to the "Prairie Rose" bungalow. I can't wait to see what you've done to it," said Diana to Caroline.

"To answer your question Marti, our Ms. Sigrid is not with me. I was paged at the airport and she told me her flight had been delayed...seems she's flying in from Palm Springs. She told me to go ahead without her."

"Palm Springs?" asked Caroline. "Are you sure?"

"Yes, I'm sure. She expects to be here in another hour or so," said Diana.

"Palm Springs...hmmm, maybe she and Arturo did take a little time off," said Marti.

"Who's Arturo?" asked Diana and Paula simultaneously.

Caroline winked at Carmen and said, "I think we should let Siggy tell you all about it. Let's not deny her little surprise."

"Not to mention those other little surprises that keep showing up in my refrigerator. How many dozens of those tiny pies do you each have in your freezer? Be honest...," said Caroline.

"I take them to my students," confessed Paula.

"I take them to our board meetings," added Diana.

"We serve them here weekly," said Carmen.

"I'll be interested to know what Dr. Kate has been doing with hers, since she surely cannot be taking them to her clinic," said Marti.

"I for one...am ready to admit that I indulge and eat those luscious little pies – but only once a week," said Caroline.

"Uh–huh...sure," teased Carmen. "We love them! Fortunately we have a staff that does, too. So they don't last very long around here. I think JB takes them to out to the barn. He doesn't think I notice, but I know he does.

Since Sigrid will be late and Kate is not coming until tomorrow, why don't we have dinner now? I have a new kitchen staff that is waiting to serve us."

"Sounds great to me," said Marti. "I took a peek in the kitchen about a half hour ago and it smelled delicious!"

"That – is a given!" said Caroline. "You may not know, but Carmen doesn't cook for AngelFire very often anymore. These beautiful meals she creates for our retreats are her gift to all of us."

"And we graciously give thanks for them," said Diana. "God bless the cook!"

Carmen and the kitchen staff had prepared for the travelers a simple meal of New Mexico Chile glazed chicken on paella with butternut squash and white beans to warm them after their mountain voyage. The *piece de resistance* would be the Rose Petal Cream Glacee.

"Remember last year when we tested out Chef Niccolini at our closing dinner, before we went to the concert? Well, Caroline hired him," announced Carmen. "This Roberto is one handsome man, so I don't mind sharing the kitchen at all!"

"So we've noticed," teased Caroline. "Chef Niccolini will be creating another superb dinner for us this Saturday night, when we're all together."

"So Marti, tell us about your concert schedule," said Paula.

"I feel like my career is just beginning; I'm booked for concerts at several venues in California and it looks like I will be zigzagging the state for the rest of the year. Fortunately, one engagement leads to another; someone makes a call on my behalf and another concert is booked. I hope that by next year, I can give up my day job and start traveling around the country. I've met lots of great people, most of whom are generously supportive. The folks at the Pacific Symphony have opened many doors for me. Believe me, I am very grateful. I am finally living out a dream. It's not always easy, but I'm thrilled to have the opportunity to play the music I love."

"Just don't give up composing. Erik's Theme was magnificent, and it catapulted you into where you are today. I want you to come to speak to my students and tell them about how you achieved your dream," said Paula.

"Catapulted? The truth is that it has been more like baby steps up the side of a mountain through decades of hard work. Nothing about this was ever easy for me.

Each of you knows all about living out your dreams – right?" responded Marti. "Paula, you have the Youth Orchestra, Caroline and Carmen have this gorgeous place and Diana now has a successful career as a televangelist. It all comes with sacrifice, hard work and exhilarating achievements. But sometimes, there is a price."

Caroline and Carmen looked at each other and then Carmen spoke first. "We are doing something we love and enjoy, here at AngelFire. It is our life and yes, we do work hard and have achieved a great deal. I'm not sure how exhilarating it is at the end of the day...we're too tired to think of it as exhilarating!"

Caroline added, "AngelFire was Frank's dream... I'm not sure I have any dreams anymore. Don't get me wrong, I love the Inn, and the people – especially our regulars, and we live a good life up here *in the middle of somewhere*. Sometimes success means achievement, sometimes it means fulfillment, and if you're lucky you get both."

"It is a tranquil place, this AngelFire Inn. This is what I think we all want – serenity and security. I think you both live a life surrounded by beauty and peace," said

Diana. "What more do you want?"

"Sometimes, there *is* a feeling that there is more to do," confessed Carmen. "I know that JB and I felt the thrill of an important accomplishment when the new high school was completed, and we were able to support programs that are missing in most other schools. Our community work is outside of our daily work and there is great fulfillment that comes from that. JB especially loves working with young people. Sometimes we wish we could do more, but we do not want to give up AngelFire."

"Perish the thought!" gasped Caroline. "I wouldn't even consider AngelFire without you!"

"What about you Reverend Diana? How do you like living your dream?" asked Paula.

"Well, it has often been quite a new challenge for me, being in front of the camera, instead of behind the scenes, and we've had a mixed response from our audience, vacillating from approval to disdain. Our country still has some work to do when it comes to full acceptance of women in the clergy. The good news is that our number of viewers and contributions has increased significantly. So economically, it was a good move. The fulfillment comes in being of service in ways we couldn't have imagined. The letters I've received from young women who are now considering the ministry as a vocation is truly gratifying. "

"Do you get a lot of letters?" asked Carmen.

"I get letters from people who are happy to hear what I have to say and some who think I don't know what I am talking about. I get letters from people who think I am too thin or too fat, too ordinary or too elegant, and from some who want to marry me, and hate mail from those who want me to disappear. I don't read my mail anymore.

One thing that happened this year, and that I am happy to report, is that since my part in the ministry has grown, my marriage is stronger. Jackson likes alternating the altar!" said Diana.

"That's not the only big thing that happened this year. Do you want to explain to us what happened with Miss Elaina? It happened so fast my head was spinning!" said Marti.

"Well..." started Diana, who was interrupted by the sound of voices in the entry.

"That must be Siggy!" said Caroline, who was glad for the distraction.

And in a cloud of pink, Ms. Sigrid Kerrington entered the room. She was grinning from ear to ear.

"*Hello dahlings....*"

Four gaping mouths rose to greet her. Each gazed in astonishment at the newly transformed woman before them.

"You...you look beautiful!" said Diana.

"Siggy, when?...Palm Springs? – Wow!" said Caroline.

Marti was the first to hug her friend and said, "Grandma, what big lips you have!"

"Oh, they'll recede a little by the end of the week. By Saturday they will be perfect!" said Sigrid.

"What exactly did you have done?" asked Paula.

"Well, do you want me to start from the bottom and go up, or go from the top and go down! First, I'll give you the general outline. Since I've lost almost fifty pounds, I decided I deserved a reward, so I bought myself a facelift. A little liposuction came after that. Then I went to this Botox happy hour on Thursday and well...here I am!" said Sigrid, proudly.

"Here's a glass of wine, and please sit and have something to eat," said Caroline. "We want to hear all about it."

"Well I think you look amazing," said Carmen. "I think next year, I will take a little time off and go to Palm Springs all by myself and see what can be done for me."

"Your new hair color and style are so youthful! Siggy, you never spoke about doing all this before. What made you decide to do it?" asked Caroline.

"The truth is, I have spent my whole adult life caring for children, both mine and other people's. Now I have the bakery, and for the first time in my life, I am doing something for me and my future. I have given too many years away, waiting for my husband to come back, or waiting for my kids to grow up, or waiting to win the lottery, or one of a thousand cooking contests I entered. Now I'm working hard at building something, and I will be waiting for the right time to sell. By that time, I might be too old to look this good!

One day I looked in the mirror and said to myself – 'I want ten years back, that's all'. So I said to the surgeon as I was going under... 'Okay doc, just give me back a decade."

"You got more than that," said Diana. "I think you look fabulous!"

"Thank you. Now I hope Artie will be pleased, too," said Siggy.

"You didn't tell him?" said Carmen and Caroline simultaneously.

"No, I wanted to surprise him," answered Sigrid. "Why?"

"What will you do when he passes right by you?" asked Marti.

"Do I look that different?"

"YES!" answered her friends.

"But in a good way – right?" asked Siggy.

"Of course!" said Paula, "but I need you to back up a little here and tell Diana and me, who this Artie person is."

"Well...he is...our Master Baker, and my right hand and he...he...well, he is the nicest man that I have met in a decade," answered Siggy.

Caroline raised her hand to her mouth to cover her smile, while Carmen bit her lower lip and Marti looked toward the ceiling.

Diana and Paula leaned forward and said "And?"

"And he'll be here on Saturday and you can see for yourself!"

"Why Ms. Sigrid... have you taken a lover?" teased Paula.

"I'm not sure I would say it *that* way...I think I will go unpack my luggage now and give Artie a quick call to let him know I arrived okay," said Sigrid. "I am going to meet Miss Lulu Parr, one of Buffalo Bill's cowgirls. I hope you don't mind. I am very tired and I need my beauty sleep you know. What time are we going up the mountain tomorrow?"

"Kate said she would be here by eight o'clock, so we'll have breakfast about eight-thirty tomorrow morning. Will that give you enough beauty sleep, Ms. Sigrid?" asked Caroline.

"Yes, but I always take a brisk walk about eight or eight thirty," she responded.

"Not up here you won't – remember you are at eight thousand feet," said Carmen. "I don't want my husband to have to fetch you from the hospital in Taos again."

"How could I have forgotten, after all that drama last year!" said Sigrid.

"No exertion while you are at AngelFire altitudes," said Marti.

Sigrid turned and walked away mumbling something like *"Artie's going to love that little piece of news"*.

After a fine dinner together, everyone took their wine into the great room. Each of the women also wanted to get to bed early.

Carmen bid everyone sweet dreams and returned to the kitchen to direct the staff and close up for the night.

"Are you feeling comfortable about going up that mountain tomorrow?" Diana asked Paula.

"Yes, Niki would have loved another trip up there," she answered.

"It will be cold up there; dress warmly. Remember, we'll take the tram both ways, so we will be sheltered," said Caroline, as she gave her a hug.

"Do you have any questions or is there anything else you want to talk about with me?" asked Diana.

"No, nothing...just...thank you," Paula said softly. She turned to leave the room, and then turned back. "I guess I am staying with Miss Cheyenne tonight."

With compassion and a little heartache, Caroline and Diana watched her leave the Inn, yet they both knew that...

"The salve that soothes a broken heart is often the company of a good friend."

When Diana and Caroline were alone, Caroline said, "Well, thanks to Sigrid, you dodged a bullet tonight!"

"Indeed, I did. I figured it would come up, but you know I can't talk about it. I trust these women, but a gag order is a legal commitment. You know I won't discuss anything to do with Miss Elaina," said Diana.

"I know – but we have so much going on this week, I'm not really worried; and if it does come up, I'm reasonably sure Sigrid will provide plenty of distraction. She does look great, doesn't she?"

"It makes me at least think about having a little something done here and there, maybe," said Caroline. "Wouldn't you?"

"I already have..." said Diana with a wink and a smile. "Don't ask....and good night!

Diana's Triumphant Year

"There is in every true woman's heart a spark of heavenly fire, which lies dormant in the broad daylight of prosperity; but which kindles up, and beams and blazes in the dark hour of adversity."

~Washington Irving, The Sketch Book, 1820

It had been nearly a year since the great Reverends, Jackson and Diana Greene, enjoyed a month in seclusion on a private beach on the island of Tonga, in the British Virgin Islands. It was there where they thrashed through their marital difficulties. Both revealed their fears and both opened to forgiveness and a recommitment to their future. Their lives had purpose and meaning and nothing or no one would ever impinge upon their personal mission again.

At dawn on the last morning of their sabbatical, they walked down to the beach and faced the sun. Together they renewed their commitment to each other, to their ministry, and to God. No witnesses were needed – just Diana, just Jackson, just God.

They vowed to always face the Light of Truth, for to turn away meant to stand in the shadows.

When they returned to North Carolina and to their ministry, they called a board meeting and began the plans to bring Diana to the forefront and to create a more visible program as a couple.

Some broadcasts would be done completely as a couple and others would alternate between them. The majority of the board of directors were enthusiastic about this new avenue. The skeptics took *a wait and see* stance.

At first, Diana appeared a bit nervous, but within a few weeks, her talks became stimulating and thought provoking. The media proclaimed her a success. Women all over the country began to write to her regarding their own experiences, as they put to practice some of the principles she avowed.

Caroline went for a visit in early July, which resulted in an involvement in a sequence of events that neither she nor Diana would ever have imagined. She was present for a Sunday taping of a broadcast where Diana and Jackson were acting as a team. Their message was filled with humor and Truth. Afterward, the three of them had dinner together in one of those out-of-the-way places that they used to go to years ago, when Caroline and Ric joined them as a couple. Although the restaurant provided a bit of nostalgia, the conversation was essentially focused on the future.

On the following Monday morning, Diana announced she was taking the day off to spend a little time with Caroline. She had lined up a few treatments at a day spa. They were preparing for their day and about to go out the door when both of their cell phones rang simultaneously.

Caroline answered hers first, Diana a second later.

The call on Caroline's phone was Ric, her ex-husband. "Your ears must be ringing – how did you know where I was?" she started, but he interrupted her.

Diana turned away from her and sank into the sofa. She grabbed the arm of the sofa to steady herself.

"Turn on the TV – Now!" said Ric.

"What? But we're...," started Caroline.

"Now!" repeated Ric. "I'll call you back as soon as I talk to Jackson."

Mystified, Caroline turned to see Diana with the remote in her hand. All the color had drained from her face. Caroline turned to look at the TV screen.

It appeared to be a press conference – men and microphones, reporters and one young woman. Diana turned up the volume.

"Fox News reporter Posy Peabody reporting live – Well there you have it folks. It looks like we may have yet another televangelist, with clay feet. Miss Elaina Kirkland has just filed a sexual harassment suit against Reverend Jackson Greene. This suit was filed today in Superior Court in Raleigh. It seems that she and her attorneys acted quickly to be within the one year deadline for filing this suit."

The young woman was Miss Elaina.

"She did not speak for herself, but her attorney stated that Ms. Kirkland was fired after an incident that qualified as sexual harassment. We will look forward to reporting on Reverend Greene's response," said Ms. Peabody.

Diana turned off the TV. She and Caroline sat speechless for a brief moment. Telephones and cell phones were ringing all over the house again. Diana sat silently with her eyes closed. When Caroline saw that it was Ric calling again, she got up and took the phone into the dining room.

She answered with, "What do I do?"

"You just take care of Diana. I'm in Washington DC and will be there this afternoon. I've already spoken to Jackson. You and I will be taking them somewhere away from the media. Who the hell is this woman? Jackson said she was a former organist? Do you know anything?"

"Yes, actually, I know all of it. It wasn't sexual harassment, Ric."

"This is about money. An opportunistic attorney got a hold of a young woman whose feelings were hurt, and it has been turned into an opportunity for fifteen minutes of fame and the possibility of a small fortune. I will be there by four o'clock and

Jackson, Diana, you and I will make a plan," said Ric. "The faster we move on this the better. I've already got some of my people working on it."

Caroline went back to Diana's side, and placed her hand or her friend's shoulder. "Ric is on his way here. We're going to take you away from the eye of the media." Diana looked at Caroline with tears welled in her eyes, and said "Thank you."

"Our Ric, the proverbial *'fixer'*. He has his people talking to Jackson's attorney. He said he will be here by four o'clock. We're supposed to pack our bags and to pack one for Jackson. We are going to meet and go somewhere where the media won't find us."

Diana said nothing.

The two women quietly did as they were asked. They ignored the telephone. Diana took one call on her cell phone. It was Jackson, and she went into their bedroom and closed the door to take the call.

When she returned she asked Caroline to call Ric. She took Caroline's phone into her bedroom and spoke to him privately.

"Well?" said Caroline when Diana returned her cell phone. "What are you up to?"

"Come on, let's get in the car. We'll take your rental instead of my car. Here is a hat and glasses, just in case anyone is waiting at the guard gate."

"Where are we going?" asked Caroline.

"We're meeting Jackson and Ric, but you and I are going make a little stop first," she answered.

"Geez, I feel like I just stepped into an old rerun of Cagney & Lacey. What are you thinking right now, Diana?"

"I'm thinking that if I step up and practice what I believe, I can stop this right now," said Diana, with conviction.

"What? Don't you want to hear what Ric finds out, what the attorneys say and... where are we going exactly," asked Caroline.

Diana's cell phone rang. "Really now...Who is with her? Okay, well Caroline will help manage him. We'll call you when we get there."

"Caroline will do what?"

"Caroline will pray with me right now, so that I know exactly what to do and exactly what to say. Okay, get on the Hwy 540 freeway and head for Wake Forest Road. We're going shopping."

Caroline took a deep breath and got on the freeway, as she exhaled, she looked at Diana, whose eyes were closed. *Is she really praying,* she wondered? Within minutes they were exiting onto Wake Forest Road. She was about to interrupt Diana when her cell phone rang.

"Okay, thanks Ric, we're there. We'll call you back," she said. "Saks Fifth Avenue." Diana ended the call and leaned over toward Caroline. "She's buying a new outfit for her press conference tomorrow."

"Ugh...Diana, this could be a royal disaster," said Caroline. Diana did not respond. Instead they walked briskly and took the escalator to the second floor, petites department. A tall man in dark glasses and a suit was standing by in the aisle while a young woman went through a rack of dresses. She too was wearing a hat and sunglasses.

"Offer to help her and get her into a dressing room," whispered Diana.

Caroline rolled her eyes, and walked over to the young woman. She began speaking to her softly and casually, "I'm not finding anything for me - how about you?"

"There are a couple of pretty dresses. I'm supposed to find something sweet. This powder blue one is nice...does this look sweet to you?" asked the lovely Elaina.

Caroline noted her demeanor. She seemed nervous and soft spoken, and was really quite pretty. No one had mentioned that before. Caroline picked up a dress in a pink print and said, "How about this one? Pink is always sweet, everyone likes a soft pink. But you will have to try it on, don't you think?"

Elaina signaled the man casing the aisle and pointed to the fitting rooms. Caroline followed her. "I'll stay out here and give you a second opinion if you like. I never shop without a good friend who will give me an honest opinion." Caroline wondered if her nose was growing longer. She looked around for Diana, but didn't see her. She soon figured out exactly where Diana was. Caroline remained outside, in the entry of the fitting rooms.

Elaina walked toward the very back of the narrow corridor. She had thought that she and Caroline were the only two women in the department, but all the dressing room doors were closed and locked, with the exception of the one on the very end. Elaina walked right in, hung up a few dresses and shut the door. Suddenly she realized she wasn't alone.

"Hello Elaina," said Diana.

Eyes wide open and frightened, she answered, "I'm not supposed to talk to you."

"Okay, you don't have to say anything. How about if I talk? Would that be okay? I am not here to threaten you or intimidate you, or even to question you. I think I already know what is going on here and I've come to make you an offer."

"My attorney said you would be offering me money right away. I'm not supposed to accept any offer without him being present," said Elaina as her voice was shaking.

"Oh, I'm not offering you any money. First I want to talk, and then you can answer, or accept my offer, or do whatever you want. Okay?" said Diana.

"Well make it fast, I have someone out there – a man, you know," she said.

"I know. Elaina, do you remember when you applied for the job to be an organist? You had a reference, who was a personal friend of mine. Ms. Ann Matthews – right? I called her and she said you were a fine young woman, who had grown up in her church and was very well liked. You played the organ in her church in San Leandro – right?"

Elaina nodded her head slightly.

"She also told me you had an infatuation with the choir director. I don't remember his name, but I do know that he was married. So Elaina, I am wondering if maybe a similar situation happened last summer with Reverend Greene. Jackson Greene is a handsome man, who appeals to a lot of women. You are not the first to find him attractive – in fact, so attractive his marital status seems unimportant.

I remember that day when I walked into that choir room and saw you and Reverend Greene in an embrace. I was so dumbstruck I left the building and also left a day early for a little vacation with some friends. You are a beautiful young woman and for a moment, I thought my husband was interested in you. I doubted him, I doubted our marriage, and I doubted myself.

Now, I can say what I really came here to say. I owe you an apology and my husband owes you an apology."

"What? I was...I was..." Elaina started.

"Wrong? Yes, you were. It is always important to be appropriate when you work in the ministry. And Reverend Greene was wrong, too. He should not have fired you like that. I think we were all wrong. We should not throw people away like an old magazine. I'm sorry you were tossed out of a great opportunity, with a successful ministry that could have been something important in your life. So whatever happens now, at least I had the opportunity to say what needed to be said.

Now, I'll leave you alone to buy your dress. I'm told you're a good person Elaina. I hope you will do the right thing and not lose who you are in the days ahead."

"Wait!" said Elaina. "Mrs. Greene, please wait...I only wanted my job back. I am a good church organist and well...is that possible?"

"I don't have any idea," said Diana. "I have to go now. We have a meeting with our attorneys."

Diana walked out of the dressing room and toward the shopping area.

Caroline was guarding the entry. When she saw Diana coming she said, "Hurry, I've told five women that my friend got sick and threw up all over the place. I asked them to find another fitting room somewhere else. I'm sure a maintenance person will be here any minute."

"Please wait," asked a weepy voice coming up behind them. "Can I leave with you?"

"Don't you have a man out here waiting for you?" asked Diana.

"Oh, I took care of him about five minutes ago – he's gone," said Caroline.

"What happened?" asked Diana.

"I called security and said a suspicious man was loitering in this department. It didn't take long for him to drop a few obscenities and they just took him away!"

Diana turned to Elaina, "Are you sure you want to do this?"

"Yes," she answered with her voice quivering.

"Caroline, I'd like you to meet Miss Elaina Kirkland. She is coming with us."

And the rest is history – not written, not taught, not even spoken of.

A Very Different Trip to the Mountain

"Do not surrender your grief so quickly
Let it cut more deeply
Let it ferment and season you
As few human or divine ingredients can."

- Hafiz

*K*ate had arrived on time for the early breakfast as planned. She seemed happy to see everyone, but a bit subdued. Robbie had decided to go over to his condo office.

At ten o'clock seven women boarded the Chili Express tram for a private trip up to the Sangre De Christo Mountains at the AngelFire Ski Resort. They wrapped themselves in scarves, hats and sweaters. Paula carried the urn that held the ashes of her former partner, Nicole Roberts. Her somber expression was mirrored by the faces of each passenger as the tram climbed the mountain. This was a nearly silent ride – vastly different from their previous trips up the mountain, over the past thirteen years. Only sighs of appreciation for the grand vistas before them, could be heard. Twice, in recent times, death had caught them by surprise; Frank Amoroso's accident, and now Nicole's still unsolved mysterious death.

Nicole's will had specified that any worthy organs be donated to science, with her remains to be cremated and the ashes spread somewhere at AngelFire. Caroline Amoroso had been given the authority to determine the location.

Diana had prepared a brief ceremony which befitted the moment and the forty-four degree morning temperatures at the top of the mountain. After a long hot summer in North Carolina, she had some resistance to the temperature and was practically shivering. The three California women, Marti, Sigrid and Kate, had donned heavy sweaters as they also found the temperature a little too chilly for comfort.

Caroline, Paula and Carmen were not bothered in the least. The sun was shining and giant puffs of cumulous clouds were gently sailing high above them. The air was crisp and clear and fresh. They took deep deliberate breaths. Both Kate and Carmen kept an eye on Sigrid, as she had fainted due to altitude sickness the previous year. When the tram reached its destination, the seven women cautiously disembarked, two by two, followed by Paula.

Diana directed the group to an area sheltered by giant pines, where they huddled together, then privately thanked God that there had not yet been any snow. In that moment the mountain emanated the sacredness of a divine cathedral.

And so she began... "Let us stand in a circle for a few moments and breathe in the gift of this glorious morning. I would like to start with a prayer for our dear Nicole." Diana eloquently began with a traditional prayer of comfort but surprisingly concluded it with, "we welcome your presence here today, dear Nicole, and if there is anything you would like us to know, please make it obvious that we all understand it clearly." No one responded to her statement, even though each instantly recalled, without speaking of it - the still inexplicable appearance of Frank Amoroso the previous year.

And so she continued..." The Life Force of God is pulsating right here on this mountain. It advances and recedes, rises and sinks, is lifted and leveled, ebbs and flows. It provides a rhythm from which we measure time. It creates birth and death, and It is continuous and irreversible for It is always moving forward. It is both complicated and simple. There is a deep organic likeness in all of us, which establishes our oneness, with each other, with God.

Life has its seasons, and we, my friends, have moved from one mystery to another, and together again, we are looking at death...I look at it - as Life. I have stopped looking at death as the enemy. Perhaps death is an awakening, a shift in consciousness, an onward progression to becoming a being of Light. Maybe then, a woman like Nicole can affect an even grander number of people. Regardless of our varied religious affiliations, *or not*, the Light of God lifts the world, and I like to imagine Nicole as part of that Light.

Since we attended the lovely funeral service for Nicole, we are undoubtedly aware of her unstoppable drive for social justice and responsibility, in a much grander sense. We have also had a few months to feel the loss of Nicole, so I thought we could go around our little circle and identify one thing - a gift that Nicole brought to our lives...Let's keep it brief, ladies, we can reminisce in the warmth of the fireplace later.

"I'd like to begin," said Sigrid. "I would like to say that Nicole brought a renewed sense of *courage* to my life. Because of her courage for change, I was able to look at the possibility of new love in my life. Not quite the same way she did...nonetheless, a new love interest in my life!" Smiles lit up around the circle, with the exception of Paula, whose face was marked with the trail of a tear. "Thank you Niki!" Siggy called out.

"May I go next?" asked Kate and no one objected. "I would like to add that Nicole brought *gratitude* and *mindfulness* to my life - for no matter how difficult things become for me, there are always people who have far greater struggles. Often when I let myself get overwhelmed by my work, I'd come home and find one of her fundraising letters in my mailbox and I would get an attitude adjustment. While I take so much for granted, those letters allowed me to see inside the plight of others. She kept me mindful of all that I have, and the opportunities that always lay before me. Unknowingly, Nicole often helped me to stop feeling sorry for myself. "

"For me, she represented *confidence*," added Marti. "Nicole was not only willing to be of assistance to others, she was nearly always willing to take the lead. Not all of us can do that. Most of the time, I am a follower. I have rarely had the level of confidence that Nicole consistently demonstrated. Uh – so if you are here, Niki – I miss your exuberance!"

"You have confidence Marti – it's in your music," interrupted Caroline. "I've known Nicole since she was a young girl," she began. "When Ric and I separated, she vowed to keep the boys connected to the Roberts family, as much as possible. I think she was all of eighteen or nineteen at the time. I didn't give it much thought and assumed she was just reacting to the news of our impending divorce. As it turned out her level of *commitment* was *Rock of Gibraltar* solid, and that is what Niki represented to me. My sons attended every Roberts' family function, whether they wanted to or not. Her whole life – her word meant something. Niki never did anything half-way. "

"I saw Nicole as a woman who knew herself, yet was selfless. She and Paula worked with JB and me, for the building of a new high school for our people. She was driven and purposeful in every meeting. She listened to us, and to our desires. Her ideas were always geared to what was best for our children. I saw her as dynamic and *selfless*.

All eyes turned toward Paula, whose silence was heart rending. She didn't bother to wipe the new tears from her face, as she cleared her throat. "I know that you have all only known me for a year," said Paula. "And you may still be wondering about Niki and me. There have been times when even I thought I was one of Niki's projects."

Caroline and Diana exchanged a quick glance, recalling a conversation with Ric Roberts on that very subject, where the idea was suggested, but not discussed.

"She lived with such compassion - it was easy to fall in love with her. She taught her students with contagious passion. As for all her charitable organizations...She never looked at those in need as the underdog. Instead, they were the underfed, underserved, or under appreciated. She had great leadership skills, she was incredibly resourceful, and had inexhaustible energy.

But I think what I will miss the most in her, was that she gave me *hope*. She felt that every problem was just a challenge seeking an answer. She brought joy to my emotional pain, and *hope* for my physical pain. I had faith in her - she saw potential in me. For that matter, she saw greater potential in almost everyone.

I looked forward to a life filled with her creative responses to our challenges. I trusted her. I gave her parts of me no one has ever touched." Paula's voice began to quiver. Caroline and Kate, each flanking her sides, instinctively placed an arm around her shoulders.

"I know I have to take what I have learned from Niki...and somehow incorporate it into my own future. I don't know how I will do that without her." She could not say anymore.

Diana took the cue and asked Caroline for the urn. The circle of friends moved to the crest of the mountain ridge. Diana removed the top of the urn, slowly tipping the urn to the wind. Carmen began to sing an *A'shiwi* chant. Diane said, "With our deepest appreciation Nicole, we salute these gifts of your indomitable spirit - *courage, gratitude, mindfulness, confidence, commitment, selflessness and hope.* Your life was *love in action.*"

Huddled in silence, the seven women watched a slow stream of ashes give way to the wind as if they were smoke, and they never touched the ground.

About thirty feet away, stood two specters of light in the outlines of a man and a woman. They remained still... and unnoticed. The male placed his arm of light around the female, as she buried her head in his shoulder...and together...*they watched them.*

In the Meantime...

"In the meantime, in between time
Ain't we got fun? "

Lyric - Richard A. Whiting / Gus Kahn / Ray Egan

T he ride descending the mountain was a little more light-hearted than the ascent. Each woman appreciated how Nicole's life had inspired her in such diverse ways.

"I wonder how many ways my life has affected others?" said Sigrid.

"With all the children you have taken care of over the years and all your creative undertakings, I'll bet there are abundant, rich and hysterical memories whole families would love to tell about you," said Marti. "Not to mention the great and mighty wonder of my own stories."

"Don't ever underestimate the impact we have on others," said Diana. "Sometimes I get letters from people who have reacted to one sentence in a Sunday message – One sentence!"

"We never know the various ways one person can affect another," said Caroline. "All of you have had a tremendous impact on my life."

"How are you feeling, Paula?" asked Carmen, as she noticed her solemn face.

"Oh, I'm okay," answered Paula. "I'm getting used to the idea of living alone again. I'm so busy with my new concert season and my new students, that my days are pretty full. It's the nights that are hard to get through."

"Amen," said Caroline.

"Well, I have planned something special for dinner tonight for Katie. It is time for us to have some fun. We have never officially celebrated Katie's engagement to Robbie."

"Thank you, Carmen!" said Kate.

"I am ready for that!" said Sigrid. "I wish Arturo were here. He loves a good party."

"I hear he is coming up on the weekend. Is that true?" asked Marti.

"Yes, I want you all to meet him," answered Sigrid with a broad smile.

"I met Robbie last year, you met Arturo this year, I wonder who will be next?" said Kate. "Maybe a new love for Marti or Caroline?"

"HA!" both chimed in. "Unlikely, for me," said Caroline. "Maybe some fascinating tuba player is waiting in the wings for Marti!"

"Very funny," started Marti. "I don't think I would know how to live with someone else. Doesn't that scare you Katie?"

"YES! It still does...and to tell the truth, it has been quite an adjustment for both of us," she answered. "And as for all the compromises, I certainly hope it's worth it."

The Chili Express landed at its home base and the women headed back to AngelFire, where the staff had hot coffee, pastries and fruit prepared. Caroline had to take a phone call and went upstairs to her private office. Diana, Kate and Sigrid headed for their bungalows to change their clothes, while Paula followed Carmen into the kitchen.

"Would you be upset if I passed on the dinner tonight?" asked Paula. "I'd like to go home to work on my music and return for the big weekend."

"Have you mentioned this to Caroline?" asked Carmen. "I think it is important that you be with your friends and have a little fun. Please don't go, yet."

"Go?" asked Caroline, as she returned to the kitchen. "Paula, you want to leave?"

"I do," she answered. "There is so much to do and I want to rehearse with my little band for this weekend. I can leave my gift here. You can explain it for me."

"Paula, I am going to ask you to stay for the party for Katie tonight and just relax, here with your friends. I know all too well how we can bury ourselves in our work to avoid our grief. When is your rehearsal – really?" asked Caroline.

"Uh...Thursday," Paula answered, sheepishly.

"Good, then you can at least stay the night and if you want to leave in the morning...we'll all understand," said Caroline. "Paula, after I lost Frank, Carmen and JB had incredible patience with me and all I really wanted to do was stay upstairs in my apartment."

"And she had a hundred excuses to do so," added Carmen.

"You might feel like you are swimming through Jell-O right now, or driving through a San Francisco fog. Yet, I promise you, you will get through this. You will also find hope again, within yourself. The hope Nicole instilled into your life still exists within you. It doesn't have to die with her. Just give yourself time to realign with it again. You are young, alive and have a wonderful career. I am guessing that you inspire hope in your students, and you don't even realize where it's coming from. Please let us work with you, to get through this grief process. Friends are your greatest blessing for recovery."

"We watched Caroline go through it, and we will do the same for you," said Carmen. "Why don't you go change your clothes and come back and have a little lunch with me and JB? We'll tell you all kinds of stories about Caroline."

"Okay, I'll try not to be the Killjoy," answered Paula, and after a good laugh, she agreed to stay another day. She then returned to her bungalow to change and to make a few phone calls.

Caroline waited for her to leave and turned to Carmen, "That phone call was from Ric. The Santa Fe police have a lead on one of the teenagers involved in Nicole's accident. We agreed not to say anything to Paula until we have more information."

"I'm surprised he said anything to you until *he* had more information," said Carmen.

"I think he just needed to talk about it. He's not going to share this with his mother, yet." said Caroline.

"I think he just needed to talk to you. I've seen the way he looks at you Caroline," said Carmen. "He still cares about you, and before you say it – not just because you are the mother of his children."

"Geez, Carmen, when did you get to the point where you know the words before they come out of my mouth?" said Caroline laughingly.

"Oh...a couple of years ago, I think. I need to talk to JB, before we have lunch. I have a few details to take care of before tonight's party for Kate. I'll see you in about an hour, okay?"

"Make sure he has the APAC room heated for tonight," added Caroline as Carmen exited the back door.

AngelFire Performing Arts Center had become the APAC room to the AngelFire staff. They now had their very own theater, where a great many happy memories were made. This year they added better lighting and Carmen had arranged for tables and chairs for the weekend party. She was playing it safe just in case the weather didn't cooperate with their plans.

Dinner was scheduled at seven for seven friends who were ready *to let their hair down* and be drawn into each other's annual stories. Their lives had taken dramatic steps over the past year and each was anxious to share and support each other.

The AngelFire Inn was abuzz with hushed excitement as they prepared for the weekend, which would bring additional guests and maximize their occupancy. Caroline and Carmen achieved the flexibility of a yogi while coordinating their plans with the realities of mountain living. Caroline often wondered how Frank had made it all look so easy. Time had alleviated the grief of Frank's early demise, but he was the foundation of the AngelFire Inn, its creator, and his mission was their mission. Caroline saw the evidence of his dreams realized, and his labors rewarded, knowing full well that none of it had been accomplished without her partnership and those of Carmen and JB Robles. The plentitude of Frank's legacy had not only brought security and stability, but it also opened a world of possibilities for Caroline, possibilities which she had barely begun to look at.

At six-thirty, Carmen and JB joined Caroline in the dining room. They held a private toast to the accomplishments of the week and to the events about to transpire. The only missing partner in their plan was Robbie Collicci, the *"keeper of the kash"*, as nicknamed by JB. Carmen lit the candles, while Caroline placed individual gifts at each place setting, and JB stoked the fireplace. Caroline noticed that JB seemed exceptionally quiet, which may have had something to do with Carmen's pricey designer outfit and the stunning piece of jewelry around her wrist. Surely, Caroline thought, he had to admit that she looked like a million dollars!

"JB, will you stay with us for a while, and at least have dinner?" asked Caroline, already knowing his answer, but extending the invitation anyway.

"No, I'm having dinner with Robbie over at the club, tonight," answered JB.

"You are?" said Carmen.

"I'll bet Robbie needs to talk to a long-time married man for some encouragement," said Caroline.

"*Really, JB*? Do you have some good advice to give him for a long and happy marriage?" asked Carmen.

In his usual and customary way, JB withdrew quietly from the conversation. He thanked Caroline for the invitation, gave a quick peck on the cheek to Carmen, and left for the evening.

"Obviously, there is tension between you two. How can I help, so that you can get back to the Carmen and JB, we all know and love? Please let this just be a bump in the road, and work on it together, before it becomes a crossroad," said Caroline.

"I never noticed you and Frank having difficult periods like this," said Carmen. "Lately, JB makes me feel guilty about taking care of myself, and I get furious with his criticism. Things have changed here, and it is all for the better. I just don't understand his attitude," said Carmen.

"Actually, I wasn't thinking of Frank and me. I was thinking of my marriage with Ric Roberts. I used to say he had a cell phone business, a cell phone life, and a cell phone divorce. We were unable to see how we used technology as a factor to emphasize our stubbornness. I was so caught up in what he was or wasn't doing I didn't recognize my own part in it. We never sat down and figured out how to save what we once had. We didn't even try. We were not mature enough or wise enough to see what we had done to each other. The sad part was that we had two boys who were deeply affected by the divorce."

Carmen walked over to Caroline and put an arm around her shoulder. "No regrets tonight, okay? Your words are not lost on me and I promise you, JB and I will work this out. We've come too far to let this chapter end our marriage, but I might have to do some damage first."

"Damage?" asked Caroline.

"Well there is this one little thing I saw at a gallery in Taos...."

Showering Kate

"Everything that lives -Lives not alone -Nor for itself"

- William Blake

 T he ambiance of the dining room had been transformed
with soft lighting, while amber stemware, ivory china
and aubergine linens graced the table. A copper platter
was placed in the middle of the dining table and centered upon it
was a jade sculpture of Quan Yin with small fruits and orchids at
her feet to honor the Chinese influences in Kate's life and career
in Naturopathic medicine. Quan Yin, the Chinese goddess of
compassion and mercy, was a befitting tribute to a woman who
had spent her life trying to support the health and well-being
of others. Kate's compassionate care stemmed from her early
days as a nurse in Los Angeles and grew into the present with
the successful wellness center she founded in Sonoma. When
Caroline and Marti had first met Kate, so many years ago, her
compassion for Marti's circumstances and her commitment to
support her emotionally, had bonded the three of them for life.

Copper ice buckets filled with ice and champagne bottles flanked the centerpiece – for a little dose of reality. Holiness was not exactly on the party invitation. Music, laughter, gifts, wine and great food were all on the agenda. Kate had explicitly stated that she wanted no wedding showers or even wedding gifts. Her friends and associates in California respected her wishes, while her AngelFire friends ignored her request, opting for something a little more creative.

Caroline and Carmen surveyed the room for any details left undone. They smiled at each other as they realized that they had created an altogether new occasion in the thirteenth year of these retreats. They had planned several surprises for the bride to be. The truth was that there were a few surprises in store for all of them, which even Caroline and Carmen were yet to discover.

Their self-felicitations were soon interrupted, as Paula and Diana arrived. Paula placed a large white envelope on the gift table and went directly to Carmen to acquire a glass of anything she had to offer. Diana carried in a small package wrapped in natural linen. A white silk peony, secured by a black grosgrain ribbon, sat elegantly atop the gift. Her small package was dwarfed by a box about two feet tall and a foot wide that was encased in a suede drawstring bag. The drawstrings were beautifully beaded which gave away the giver of this gift.

"Is that a book on how to keep a happy marriage?" asked Carmen. "Because if it is, I think I need a copy. My husband *Ebenezer* is mad at me again, and tonight he has gone out to dinner with Robbie Collicci. I'm just glad that Robbie is not an attorney."

"Please say you don't mean that." Diana placed her gift, and she, too, secured a glass of champagne. "This is supposed to be a happy week – right?"

Paula was quietly taking in the ambiance when she turned and watched Sigrid make her entrance. She entered in a red paisley cape that hung over her shoulders and partially covered her gift box. The box was completely covered in peach and white satin ribbons woven together, and much too beautiful to unwrap. Sigrid was singing the lyric *"Goin' to the chapel, and we're – gonna - get ma- a- arried – going to the chapel of love."* She sashayed over to the gift table and continued her sashaying over to the dining table, where she slung her cape over a chair, revealing her stunning red jumpsuit.

"Wow – Wow – Wow!" chimed in the others.

Caroline handed Sigrid a glass of champagne, took her other hand and said, "I can't get over how beautiful you look. You will share with us, the name of this magical place you went to in Palm Springs – right?"

"Of course, I will – eventually..."

"So were you singing that song for Kate or for yourself?" asked Carmen.

"What's this? Sigrid has a new love?" asked Diana.

"I guess I can say that," answered Sigrid.

"Is this serious or are you just having a little fun?" asked Paula.

"At your age, you can ask that question....at my age, it's more than just a little fun."

"Really? Okay, sounds like you have a plan."

"I do."

"You do?" said Caroline, Carmen and Diana simultaneously.

"You do what?" asked Marti as she walked into the dining room. Caroline handed Marti a champagne flute and took her neatly wrapped gift box – in white on white striped paper with Kate's monogram in a Gaelic symbol centered on the front, and placed it on the gift table.

"She has a plan," said Carmen.

"Do you want to share this plan?" asked Marti.

"Actually, I do not...This is Kate's night."

"Where is Kate by the way?" asked Diana.

"She must be with Robbie, in the May Lillie bungalow," answered Caroline.

"I don't think so, I thought I heard a car leave from their place about a half an hour ago," said Marti.

"That could have been JB. He left some time ago to meet Robbie for dinner at Stonewood," answered Carmen.

"I thought the car came from Kate's place, but I could be wrong."

Sigrid cleared her throat, and added, "Ladies, since we know that they were together...perhaps they were *together-together* and our Kate may just be rearranging her hair or putting on fresh makeup...you know."

"Oh...okay then, let's have the hors d'oeuvres served now and we'll just give her a little more time," said Carmen, as she looked over to Caroline, who shrugged her shoulders. "Chef Niccolini has prepared a light dinner for us tonight as kind of a preview of the sumptuous dinner he is preparing for us on Saturday."

"I don't think Kate will mind, so I would like to propose a toast to our hosts and wedding planners extraordinaire....Caroline and Carmen," said Diana.

"I don't know how you pulled all this together, with all of us so far away from each other," added Sigrid.

"How much does Katie know?" asked Marti.

"She and Robbie picked the date and agreed to have the wedding here," said Caroline. "You have each played your own part, which made it all pretty easy."

"There is nothing easy about planning a wedding," said Diana. I've seen some pretty strange happenings. Sometimes by the time the wedding date arrives it's like the Hatfield's and the McCoy's!"

"Caroline just makes it look easy, and we thank you for the toast. We think this is going to be a wonderful wedding that she will remember forever," said Carmen.

"They know nothing else?" asked Paula.

"Who went with her to shop for her wedding dress?" asked Diana. "A bride needs her friends with her for that."

"I did...I went with her for the dress," said Marti.

"You did?" said Sigrid. "When?"

"She made an impromptu trip down to LA. We tried calling you – but you, and it seems Arturo, were not answering your phones."

"Oh...yes, well sometimes you just have to turn them off, you know."

"And Kate is well aware of that. She says when Robbie comes to Sonoma; they both at least silence the ringers on their phones, too. It was a marathon sprint, shopping at several carefully chosen little shops, where she tried on about forty dresses. It was a quite an experience. She went home the same day. I was exhausted!"

Carmen refilled everyone's glasses and slipped away to call Kate's bungalow. There was no answer. As she turned to walk toward the dining room, she found Caroline heading her way.

"Did you reach her?"

"No, which must mean she is on her way over here."

"Then let's have the salads served. She'll be here in a minute." Caroline decided to meet Kate on the path toward her bungalow as it was already getting dark. They met about halfway, and Caroline put her arm around Kate's shoulder. "You're missing a great dinner party; we're one glass of champagne ahead of you!"

"Sorry, I'm late. I had to touch up my face. Love the May Lillie, Caroline...lots of character. I think Robbie was a little intimidated by the artwork of women with rifles, though."

Caroline walked in behind Kate as they entered the dining room. She caught a look of concern on Marti's face.

Carmen was waiting with a flute of the bubbly and handed it to Kate she said, "Drink up! You have some catching up to do!"

Kate perused the dining table and her eyes went right to the Quan Yin centerpiece. "Where did you find this beauty? This is absolutely exquisite! How did you get the baby orchids up here in AngelFire?" She looked further around the room and noticed the gift table. Tears welled up in her eyes and she said, "Oh my goodness, this is a party for me, isn't it? I might have known you would ignore the no gifts rule." She thanked everyone profusely, then sat down to take it all in.

Marti threw an inquisitive look over to Caroline. Both of them knew something was amiss.

A salad of olives, artichoke hearts, grilled red peppers and homemade mozzarella balls on a field of greens and Italian herbs was promptly served. The champagne was switched to a Sangiovese from Tuscany, Italy. Crusty artisan breads and small bowls of tapenades accompanied the salad. Next, a steaming hot Cioppino was carefully placed in front of each place setting.

"Uh... she said, just a little light supper; a soup and salad," said Marti. "This is gorgeous!"

"Just so you know, we don't eat like this every day," said Carmen. "We have Chef Niccolini for a few days, so we asked him to make something simple for tonight. We know that whatever he does it will be *delizioso.*"

"Well, I for one am completely delirious. It seems I've eaten nothing but lettuce for the last six months and this looks amazing! Just keep my portions small, so I don't have to feel too guilty!" said Sigrid.

"Amen to that!" said Diana, "This is more than enough for me. Katie, will you tell us about the dress or do you want to keep it a secret?"

"It was so hard to make a decision," started Kate.

"Now that's an understatement," interrupted Marti.

"I decided on a simple vintage dress in ecru satin and antique lace. The lines are simple, and the trims are minimal. It has a short bolero-styled jacket, that I thought would be best up in the mountain air," said Kate.

"Well it sounds lovely, and I know you will make a radiant bride," said Diana.

"Thank you," Kate answered, though there was nothing radiant about her in the moment. This did not go unnoticed by her friends.

"I wore jeans at my wedding," said Carmen.

"You did?" said Caroline.

"Yes, JB and I kind of eloped. We had a Zuni ceremonial wedding after we returned. My father would not recognize our first wedding."

"Ric and I eloped, too. We ran off to Las Vegas, much to the chagrin of my parents. My sister Julia had the grand church wedding in Bloomfield Hills, with everything and everyone we ever met. It was quite an ordeal," said Caroline. Diana took notice and thought it interesting that Caroline did not mention her wedding with Frank Amoroso. She took that as a sign that the pain of mourning the loss of him was lessening.

"Jonathon and I had a formal wedding at a hotel. I think my daddy broke the bank. I had eight bridesmaids, four flower girls, and four little boys who walked with them. One of them was the ring bearer. Somehow the rings got loose and went rolling down the aisle and under a couple of pews. Everything was stopped, and it took us ten minutes to locate them and restart the service. Looking back I think it was probably an omen, a warning that I should have really stopped the service and just walked away!" said Sigrid.

"Jackson and I had a garden wedding, at my parent's home in Florida. It was quite the elegant affair. I think Jackson was way more hesitant about going through with it than I was. I was the dreamy-eyed bride, until about three months after the wedding, and then I wondered why in the world did I get married while I was still so young? At least today young women are waiting longer."

Paula and Marti looked at each other, shrugged and said, "Shall we bring out our gifts?"

Kate remained silent.

Caroline said, "Let's have a little dessert, first. Would anyone like some coffee or tea?

"Or more champagne?" asked Carmen, which aroused a positive response, and flutes were filled. Each declined a dessert.

Caroline decided to move things along and began with, "Katie, we're all thrilled for you and Robbie, and of course you had to know we couldn't let this wedding just happen without our being a part of it, so we each have a gift for you."

"Really, everyone, I'm grateful, but I..." started Kate.

"Bite your tongue, there is nothing you can do about it! Just let us show you how happy we are for you! Paula, do you want to go first?" suggested Caroline.

Paula handed Kate the large envelope, which she proceeded to open. Inside it was a copy of the sheet music for Mendelsohn's "Wedding March" along with a hand written note. "I have arranged for a cellist, Camille MacArthur, to play this traditional wedding piece for the ceremony. I am also bringing six of my students, as we now have a little performance group that travels to promote the Albuquerque Youth Orchestra. We will also be playing some very cool dance music for the reception."

"Reception?" said Kate. "I thought the wedding was just going to be us?" Kate gave Caroline a doe-eyed quizzical glance then turned back to Paula and said, "Paula this takes my breath away! Thank you. This is incredible!"

"Since we've revealed the reception, I would like to give you my gift," said Sigrid.

"How can I open this without disturbing the ribbon? Siggy, you must have taken hours to do this. It is so beautiful!" said Kate.

"I'm a crafter – remember? Look underneath, there's a Velcro opening."

Kate gingerly moved the ribbons and opened the box, inside was a framed 8x10 photo of a large wedding cake. "Are you making the wedding cake?" asked Kate.

"No, Arturo is. He is a master at this and for some reason he insisted on using his own recipe. I had several really good ideas, but he insisted and I gave in."

"*Thank Arturo for us all*," whispered Marti under her breath.

"He's bringing it up here on Saturday," said Sigrid.

"Siggy, this is such an elegant cake, and I thank you for it, but it won't be as big as the one in the picture will it? I mean it is only, just us – Right?"

"Uh...well...there will be a few more people," confessed Caroline. "I'd like to give you a little gift from me." Quickly avoiding further questions, she handed Kate a small box which held inside a gold necklace with a jade butterfly pendant.

"The Legend of Love," said Kate. "It's so delicate, Caroline. Thank you so much."

"Of course, I want you to have the Quan Yin, too," added Caroline.

"They're both wonderful, Caroline," said Kate. "I don't know how I can thank you – all of you."

"My gift will bring you back to New Mexico," said Carmen as she brought the suede bag to the table. Kate had to stand as she unwrapped this gift. Carmen helped her pull a large handmade Zuni Wedding Vase out of the box. It was obviously a treasured collector's piece.

Kate read the attached card which said "Handcrafted by Rosa Loya", a name Kate recognized from Robbie's art collection.

"Oh my, Carmen – this is too much! Robbie has a fine collection of pottery but not one of these. I love the soft colors! Where did you find this?" asked Kate.

"I found it at the Pueblo, where my family lives. JB and I went for a visit a few weeks ago. I love the symbolism of two separate spouts coming from one pot. It is a good reminder, for me, when I look at mine. Lately, we have been drinking from separate pots, but I know we really are one. We are much stronger when I remember this."

"Robbie will love this, too. Thank you, Carmen. It really is beautiful."

Marti placed her package on the table to be opened next. "And this one is a time traveler. It's from me and Erik. Creating this gift has initiated a real healing for us."

"Oh, I am so glad to hear that," said Diana.

"How about his relationship with Erik Sr., anything new there?" asked Sigrid.

"He is actually with his father as we speak. He's doing some graphics work for his firm, and he's getting to know his half-brother, William. Erik invited him and the family to Sweden."

"I see his fine work is even on this wrapping," said Kate as she tried not to tear or crease the paper while opening it. The package revealed a green, leather bound album, with the same Gaelic symbol and monogram on the front. In it were old photos that included Kate, Marti, and Caroline from their UCLA days. There were photos of each them holding baby Erik. There was Erik's first day in Siggy's Sunday School class and a few at Mrs. Kerrington's Day Care, showing off his art projects. Most were photos that Kate didn't know existed or had long forgotten, and yet brought many a memory and much laughter. Lots of comments bandied about the room like – *Look at that outfit! What was up with your hair?* Neither Paula, nor Carmen or Diana appeared in the album, but they enjoyed it nonetheless.

When the laughter subsided a bit, Diana placed her package in front of Kate, and said, "I'm not the crafter Sigrid is, but I did make this for you."

Kate carefully opened the package to find a book titled, "*Blessings for a Marriage*". Inside were handwritten prayers, blessings, notes and quotations. Tears welled up in Kate's eyes, as she read a few lines.

"Now I know that no two marriages are alike, and all I can offer you is what I know and feel has worked for Jackson and me. Jackson and I have decided to perform the wedding ceremony together and he will arrive sometime on Friday afternoon."

"You have all been so kind. *Both of you at my wedding service?* I can't believe this," she said as she began to sob.

Marti put her arm around her and asked, "Are you okay? Was it the photo of your wild curly '70's hair?"

Kate lifted her head and said, "What you don't know is that I had an argument with Robbie tonight and told him that I wanted to call the whole thing off."

The involuntary gasps that came from Caroline and Carmen reflected the thousand things they would have to do to cancel this wedding.

"Katie," started Diana, quite calmly..."I get these calls from over half of the weddings we do. Let's talk about this for a moment. Let's make sure this is for the right reasons."

Caroline and Carmen slowly exhaled, but their knees were like jelly and they both fell back into their seats. Paula's face was in her hands. Sigrid stood straight up – her face was nearly as red as her jumpsuit.

"I know exactly why you want to cancel this wedding. You're terrified! We are part of a generation of women who grew up with mothers in traditional roles. We broke the molds, pierced the glass ceilings and became the exceptional women we are today.

It wasn't easy and we have earned every bit of independence we possess. We have become our own authority. But life is about relationships, which is exactly why we each strive to keep these friendships. Relationships don't die because there isn't any life left in them, they die because of an unwillingness or fear to try and keep trying.

Look at Caroline and Paula; they are like two little birds, each with a broken wing. They were in relationships that were working beautifully and that were taken away from them. And right now you are just too afraid to fly."

Paula looked ruefully over to Caroline, and for a moment both women felt naked in their grief.

Sigrid continued, barely skipping a beat, "Marriage for us at this stage of the game is our deepest challenge and greatest risk. This takes courage Katie O'Neil, who on Saturday evening will become Katie O'Neil-Collicci. You've faced far worse things than a man who loves you and who you were simply *"gaga"* over the moment you met him.

Also at this stage of the game, you are not getting married out of need or dependency, but because you are willing to make a commitment to LOVE. Love in a way you have not yet experienced in this life. This is not like loving your work, or your friends, or your cat. This is about growing your soul, and living authentically. You're both brilliant at what you do and you *are* ready to take the step into mature intimate love, and the fulfillment that this kind of love can bring."

Without even taking a breath, she said, "It's not going to be perfect, you cannot control it, and it won't be free of conflict. But you will grow in ways you've not yet dreamed of or discovered. And I for one – am not going to let you walk away from this. I am your friend, as we all are, and Robbie Collicci may be the best thing that has happened to you in a very long time. So Katie, if I have to walk you down the aisle myself to get you to do this, I will."

After an awkward moment of silence, Diana placed her hand on Kate's and said, "Well then Katie, I happen to agree with her.

If we didn't all think this was a good match, we'd be at this same table trying to talk you out of this marriage, but the choice is still yours. Do you want to sleep on it?"

Kate took a long slow deep breath, as tears rolled down her face. "Actually, I think I need to make a call...to apologize to my fiancé. If you will, please excuse me for a few minutes won't you?" She rose from the table and quietly left the room and walked back to her bungalow.

Dazed, Marti said, "Where did all that come from Reverend Sigrid?"

"I read a lot," she answered. "And not just recipes."

"Apparently not!" said Marti.

"Do you have any idea how many times I wished I could have given that speech?" said Diana. "You have to be pretty close to someone to have such honest dialogue all like that."

"Dialogue or lecture?" asked Marti.

"Well it produced the results we all wanted to hear didn't it? So it worked for me!" cheered Paula.

"I think I need another glass of wine. She just scared me to death!" said Carmen.

Caroline added, "We just want them to have a nice life and be happy together." She turned to Sigrid and asked "Do I really look like a little bird with a broken wing?"

"Not this year," she answered.

"Okay, Carmen, pour just a half of a glass for me, too," added Caroline.

"Who would like to play some music?" asked Marti.

"Me!" said Paula. "Come on, it will be good for all of us. Katie can meet us over there."

The company of friends picked up their glasses for a quick toast "To Love – and the O'Neil-Collicci Wedding!'" and then headed over to the APAC room. Most of it had been cleared out and was yet to be set up for the reception. Marti took the piano and Paula picked up a guitar. After a few minutes of turning on and tuning up together, Paula began with the memorable opening chords to:

Love, Love, Love.
Love, Love, Love.
Love, Love, Love.

There's nothing you can do that can't be done.
Nothing you can sing that can't be sung.
Nothing you can say but you can learn how to play the game.
It's easy.

Nothing you can make that can't be made.
No one you can save that can't be saved.
Nothing you can do but you can learn how to be you in time.
It's easy.

All you need is love.
All you need is love.
All you need is love, love.
Love is all you need.

All you need is love.
All you need is love.
All you need is love, love.
Love is all you need.

Nothing you can know that isn't known.
Nothing you can see that isn't shown.
Nowhere you can be that isn't where you're meant to be.
It's easy.

All you need is love.
All you need is love.
All you need is love, love.
Love is all you need.

All you need is love (All together, now!)
All you need is love. (Everybody!)

All you need is love, love.
Love is all you need (love is all you need)
(love is all you need) (love is all you need)
(love is all you need) Yesterday (love is all you need)
(love is all you need) (love is all you need)

Yee-hai!
Oh yeah!
love is all you need, love is all you need,
love is all you need, love is all you need,

All were singing and back into the merriment of the night. Kate walked in without being noticed, with a bit of a sheepish smile. Caroline waved her over to join them.

As the song finished, Marti asked, "Does the bride have a request?"

"I do, and this kind of tells our story."

She whispered to Marti, who smiled and started the intro to...

"Well, he walked up to me,
And he asked me if I wanted to dance.
He looked kinda nice,
And so I said, "I might take a chance."

When he danced he held me tight.
And when he walked me home that night,
All the stars were shining bright,
And then he kissed me.

Each time I saw him,
I couldn't wait to see him again.
Each time I saw him,
I couldn't wait to see him again.
I wanted to let him know,
That he was more than a friend.
I didn't know just what to do,

So I whispered, "I love you."
And he said that he loved me too,
And then he kissed me.

He kissed me in a way,
That I've never been kissed before.
He kissed me in a way,
That I wanna be kissed forevermore.

Again, all the women sang along, shaking their tambourines and all...

I knew that he was mine,
So, I gave him all the love that I had.
And one day he took me home,

To meet his mom and his dad. ("Brothers, actually" – Katie interjected)

Then he asked me to be his bride,
And always be right by his side.
I felt so happy I almost cried.
And then he kissed me.
And then he kissed me.
And then he kissed me

"I thought you would sing the Faith Hill song "This Kiss". You've always said there was something about Robbie's kiss," said Marti.

"We'll see what kind of shape I'm in at the reception. Maybe we can sing it then."

"Let's not embarrass the poor guy in front of his brothers," said Carmen.

"His brothers? Are *they* coming to the reception?" asked Kate.

"Yep and let's zip it," answered Caroline with an elbow to Carmen's ribcage.

"Oops, sorry!" she said running her forefinger and thumb across her lips.

"Reverend Diana, *doest thou havest* a song for us tonight?" asked Marti.

"No, not tonight, I'm getting a little tired," she answered.

"Me, too" said Sigrid. "That was fun, though. We'll have plenty of time for singing at the reception. Arturo is quite the drummer, too. He may want to set in with your band."

"I can't wait to meet this guy," said Paula. "Hey, I have a song. I am using a Lennon- McCartney theme for the Youth Orchestra this year. I've been working on one for myself that I love. Would you like to hear it?"

"Of course! Do you want me to play along?" asked Marti.

"No, I'll just use this guitar. She changed guitars and began to play..."

Yesterday,
All my troubles seemed so far away,
Now it looks as though they're here to stay,
Oh, I believe in yesterday.

Suddenly,
I'm not half the girl I used to be,
There's a shadow hanging over me,
Oh, yesterday came suddenly.

Why she
Had to go I don't know, she wouldn't say.
I said,
Something wrong, now I long for yesterday.

Yesterday,
Love was such an easy game to play,
Now I need a place to hide away,
Oh, I believe in yesterday.

Why she
Had to go I don't know, she wouldn't say.
I said,
Something wrong, now I long for yesterday.

Yesterday,
Love was such an easy game to play,
Now I need a place to hide away,
Oh, I believe in yesterday.
Mm-mm-mm-mm-mm-mm-mm.

"There's the bird with the broken wing," said Sigrid.

Tears rolled down Caroline's cheeks and were welled in the eyes of the others.

"Beautiful, Paula," said Diana, "Goodnight, everyone."

Caroline went to Paula, placed her arms around her and whispered, "I miss her, too"

Marti and Katie said their goodbyes and headed toward their bungalows. Paula followed behind them.

"That was you, two years ago," said Carmen to Caroline.

"And I love you for getting me through it all. I haven't got the heart to tell Paula about Ric's call. He said they're getting close to solving this case."

"Let's wait. Nothing will bring her back. Let's wait until after the wedding, although, I almost thought there wasn't going to be one!" Carmen and Caroline walked arm in arm back to the Inn.

About twenty feet behind them, stood two specters of light in the outlines of a man and a woman. They remained still, barely perceptible. The male placed an arm of light around the female, as she buried her head in his shoulder and again together, with great tenderness...*they watched them.*

Reservations at Stonewood

"A large income is the best recipe for happiness I ever heard of."

- Jane Austen

J B arrived at Stonewood and was greeted by the maître d, who directed him to the bar where he found Robbie, who was being served a second, or more likely a third, martini. They greeted each other with a handshake and rather than proceeding to the dining room, JB joined him at the bar and ordered a club soda with lime. "I don't drink; although, my wife may soon drive me to."

"I hear you JB. Women can be such a mystery," said Robbie.

"I used to think I knew my wife – inside and out," said JB. "Now she is constantly surprising me, and I get agitated pretty regularly these days." JB watched Robbie down his drink all too quickly, so he added, "I'm pretty hungry. Do you mind if we get our table and have some dinner?"

"Good idea," answered Robbie. The two men made their way to the dining room and were seated at a table where they could speak more privately, and then both ordered ridiculously oversized steaks. JB had always perceived Robbie as a quiet, reserved and wise man, whom others often sought for advice. Now, here on this night, they appeared to be on more common ground. It seemed that their women had them both confused and frustrated.

"Can I tell you something in confidence, JB?"

"Of course," responded JB, rather stone-faced. For an instant, he noted how much Robbie seemed like Frank Amoroso. Not physically, but in his manner. Frank had often asked JB to keep a confidence, in a similar manner.

"Katie wants to call off the wedding...wow, it must be the martinis...I can't believe I said it out loud. I adore this woman and I was sure she felt the same about me. Now, just a couple of days before our wedding, she wants to call it off!"

JB was stunned by this information and, as one of the three guardians of the secrets and surprises planned for the wedding, he could only image the shock that Carmen and Caroline would feel as Kate told them. In the moment, all he could muster up was, "Women! I wish I could give you an answer man. Do you have any idea why she wants out of this marriage?"

"I don't understand. She said several things, but I know that part of it has something to do with money."

"Santa Madre! Money? Now, I'm really confused. Money? What is it that money does to people? Robbie, this is why I asked you to have dinner with me. My wife and I seemed happier before we started making so much more money. Now, we argue about it all the time," JB lamented.

"Frank was right," said Robbie. "This is part of why he kept his finances so clandestine. He didn't want to have to explain anything, and he didn't want it to corrupt his and Caroline's relationship."

"Well, it is definitely eroding my marriage," said JB

"Frank and I grew up watching what money can do to people. We lived in a city where all sides of people and their money issues were played out in public. At first, when we broke away from the family business, we didn't want anything to do with the family money anymore; but that's a complicated story, and we won't be discussing it tonight," said Robbie. "My first wife married me for money and then left me for someone who she thought had more money. I don't know if he did or not, but he lavished it on her and that made her feel like she was loved more. So she left me....But, that was a very long time ago.

Katie is just the opposite and she doesn't care about money at all, either way. I just don't understand how money all of a sudden, became an issue."

"Caroline seems to be handling her newfound wealth all right," said JB. "She's still working, running the Inn and acting as if not much has changed."

"Caroline is still in denial about it. She can't handle anymore change yet, but eventually, she will. It's predictable. She still needs more time," said Robbie. "She's trying to be responsible, yet as many people do, her eyes often glaze over when we have a finance meeting. She still depends on me to make many of the decisions. She understands; she's just very agreeable."

"Your wife is having a little fun, that's all, and it will wear off, eventually. It's your own relationship to money that's causing your agitation over what she is spending. She earns that money, believe me. Carmen is just expressing a little financial freedom, and she is taking care of herself. What about you? What does money represent to you?" asked Robbie.

"To tell you the truth, I haven't given it much thought. It is hard for me, as I see my family and others at the Pueblo, struggling. I'd like to help them, but I can't support all of them. I grew up in poverty, so I was grateful that I could do my job and just pay my bills. I was content, just the way things were. Frank helped us buy a house in Taos and we have the house on the AngelFire property, too. I have a good job with people I care about, so I think I live a great life," said JB. "Why can't she be satisfied with things the way they were?"

"I think that Carmen is just trying to play catch up and is buying the things she'd previously denied herself. She's not a complainer JB, but it doesn't mean she didn't want the things she's buying now," said Robbie.

"What about you? Are you spending any of your new money?"

"Hell no – Carmen is spending enough for both of us! I save mine."

"Really? That's a fine new truck you drove over here," said Robbie.

"We both bought new wheels," said JB. "My wife thinks of money like monopoly money. I think it's a game for her! Every time she gets a check, she goes shopping. She has a new BMW, new wardrobe, a jewelry collection, and now has started an art collection. She looks like a million bucks every time she moves out the door, and she has new ideas for every room in our home."

"Katie won't let me buy her a new car. Go figure that one out," said Robbie. "Maybe that's why I am so in love with her. I understand so little about what she does for a living, and she doesn't even want to know anything about what I do. She is all about service and healing people. I love that about her. But for some reason, tonight she thinks this is why we're not a match. I don't know, maybe she thinks I will want to change the way she does business.

After all Caroline and Carmen's planning, and probably yours, too, she is calling it off. I thought she loved me, in the same way I love her. I guess I was wrong again."

"I'm sorry, Robbie. No one saw this coming. Do you think she may just have a case of the wedding jitters? Doesn't everyone get that just before they get married?" asked JB, searching for some reasonable explanation to console Robbie. JB had hoped that Robbie would consider counseling Carmen and him and put them on the road to sound financial planning. He also wanted Robbie to give him the words to convince Carmen that this would be a great idea. Yet as he saw the sorrowful look on Robbie's face and his obvious broken heart, he knew that this was not the night to ask for anything.

JB's thoughts were again turned toward the angst the news of the cancelled wedding would cause Carmen, after all her hard work and not to mention the money Caroline may just have squandered.

Switching to coffee drinks with dessert, the conversation became a little more hushed. Robbie was willing to switch topics from Katie to Frank.

"When Frank and I lived in Las Vegas, we would often see people who would win big at the tables and head straight for the nearest jewelry store. They'd blow most of their winnings, and then go home and be remorseful for what they *"could-a-should-a"* have done with it. And then – They'd come back over and over again to try to win it back. Pretty crazy – huh? Back then, we were so used to seeing this, we found it funny. After all, that kind of behavior supported the family business.

It was a difficult decision for us to leave Las Vegas, and it caused quite a conflict in our family. Since I managed the money for the family business, it was considered a crisis. It was because there were too many secrets that I had to leave behind. Frank was not like his brothers, and he and I decided this together. You don't leave a family like ours very easily. We had to make several compromises to make it all work. We came here because no one knew who we were. We were just an accountant and a slot-machine salesman. We kept our agreements with the family until both parents were gone. Then Frank met Caroline, and he decided to put our past completely behind him. They were so in love, nothing else mattered," said Robbie.

"JB, some people live for money and some are even killed for money. There are many men whose moods are leveraged by their bank balance. We hear daily reports on the stock market and economy. Today, most people worry about money. The time is coming for all of us to look at our relationship to money and how much power we give to it. I've spent my whole adult life helping people's money make even more money. And just when you think you've seen it all....someone comes along and shows you the insignificance of money.

It will make a difference in your marriage if you realize that your irritation with Carmen's spending habits has much more to do with your attitudes about money rather than hers. After this mess with Katie blows over, I'll sit down with both of you and we'll work something out. You'll be fine."

A big piece of cherry pie was placed in front of each of them and they had more coffee. Halfway through the delectable pie the maître d' came to the table and asked Robbie to come to the lobby.

"Sir, we have a telephone call for you. It is a woman and she sounds upset. Would you like to use the office? It will be much more private."

"Yes, thank you." Robbie supposed the most upset person to call him would be Caroline, who would ask him *"to do something"*. Instead, the call was from Kate.

"Robbie, I am so sorry. I know I hurt you tonight. I'm so very sorry," she said, sobbing.

"I'm sorry, too Katie. I thought this would have worked. Are you flying out tomorrow?"

"No, I'm not. I...I...I want us to get married on Saturday just as we planned."

Stunned, Robbie asked, "Are you sure?"

"No, I'm not. I'm terrified. At least those are the words my friends used to describe what's happening to me. I don't know how to do this, Robbie, but I do know that I love you. Can you forgive me? I know this has been a terrible night. Will you come back and stay with me tonight? I...I can't believe I'm saying this but – I need you tonight."

"Katie, you've never said that to me before. You need me?"

"I think that may be what I am most afraid of....needing you too much. It probably doesn't make any sense to you. Will you come back here tonight Robbie?"

"If you're sure, Katie....yes,...yes, I will. Is your dinner party over with already?"

"No, not quite. Is JB still there with you?"

"Yes, he is."

"I hope you didn't tell him what a fool I've been."

"Of course not. We're just having an enjoyable dinner, tonight."

"Okay, well can you be here in another hour?"

"Probably half that – okay?"

"Good, then we can talk more, when you get here. I truly am sorry, Robbie."

"I love you, Katie O'Neil."

"Thank you, Robbie. I needed that, too."

Robbie finished the call and went back to the table and asked the waiter for their check.

JB asked, "Well was that good news or bad news? I can't tell."

"Katie wants to get married on Saturday as planned. I'm going back to the Inn to talk to her."

"Congratulations! You can bet there's a few more sighs of relief going around the AngelFire Inn tonight." As the waiter brought the check to the table, JB quickly snatched it and placed a credit card in it, "Hey, I'll get this one. It's only a little paper, right?"

An Unexpected Guest

"Life is what happens when you are busy making other plans"

— John Lennon

Caroline was in her office at 6:00 am. With a little trepidation balanced with a little optimism, she resumed the wedding arrangements as originally planned. She knew Robbie had returned to Kate's bungalow just before midnight and that most likely they would emerge later than usual this morning. *No doubt they talked for hours*, she thought. At 8:00 am she started making telephone calls. An unexpected call rang on her private line. She answered it without noticing the Caller ID.

"Good Morning," she answered casually.

"Well, hi there, sunshine," said the caller. "I wasn't sure I would be able to reach you. Do you have a few minutes?"

"Ric? Actually, I am finishing the last details for an important wedding."

"Anyone I know?"

"It's Kate O'Neil. Do we need to talk now?"

"Kate? That's wonderful! Do you have room for one more guest?"

"Seriously? Well, I guess so if you would share a room with Brad or Jarrod."

"The boys will be there? Excellent! Then please count me in."

"That's not what you called for, is it?"

"No, but we can talk about it after the wedding. Will Paula be there?"

"Yes and so will the Greenes. Jackson and Diana will be officiating the service."

"Great! This will certainly be a pleasurable weekend – *family and friends*! Are you sure it is okay? I don't want to create a problem with table arrangements or anything."

"This is AngelFire Ric, not DC...this will all be fairly simple. Is there anything else I should know?"

"Not now. Thanks, Caroline. I'll look forward to seeing you... and everyone else, of course.

I'll fly up with the boys."

"Good... okay, I've got a million things to finish here. If there's nothing else...then we'll see you Friday. The service will be just before sunset on Saturday."

"Beautiful – Right.... I'd better call the boys."

"Ric...? Is this about Nicole?"

"Not yet, but we're close."

Caroline refused to let her heart go into that painful place that grieved for Nicole. She had a wedding to deliver.

Now I wonder what other surprises are in store for this wedding, she pondered.

Our Blonde Bombshell

"Never underestimate the power of a woman."

Ladies Home Journal – 1941

*A*t 8:45 am the phone rang in Caroline's office again.

"Are we still having our meeting after breakfast this morning?"

"Siggy? Do we...oh yes, I see it right here on my calendar. You and I are supposed to have a quarterly meeting with Robbie this morning," said Caroline. "I haven't heard from either Kate or Robbie yet this morning, so let's tentatively plan on it, based on the aftermath of last night's heart-to-heart. No one has told me to stop anything yet, so I intend to keep moving forward. Do you have anything urgent that needs to be reported?"

"Nothing critical, but there are a couple of important things I would like to discuss," said Sigrid.

"Okay, then bring your documents to breakfast at 9:00 am, and we'll see if Robbie is still willing to meet with us today, or if not, we'll have to reschedule," said Caroline.

"I believe there *will* be a wedding as scheduled," said Sigrid firmly.

"Have you become this year's Madame Zara?"

"I think we both know that Kate may have been fearful last night, but I think Robbie's a man who knows how to get what he wants," said Sigrid. "He's been single for a long time, and I'm guessing he's crazy about her and he will *make* this happen."

"Really? You're the one who seems to know how to make things happen," said Caroline.

"Uh – huh...that's interesting coming from you. You're the dream maker in this group!"

"*I – of myself – do nothing,*" mumbled Caroline. "To change the subject for a moment, Carmen and I had planned a Spa Day for everyone, today. Some of the massage therapists are already here. If we do have our meeting this morning, we'll just have to join the others later."

"I'm not sure I can do a Spa Day so soon after my surgery," said Siggy. "I will call my *Dr. Smoothface'* office and see what they suggest."

"You're not going to tell me who you went to – are you," said Caroline.

"All in good time...see you at breakfast!"

At 9:00 am the AngelFire staff presented a breakfast buffet in the dining room. Marti, Carmen and JB were sitting at a table with their coffee, waiting for the others. Paula came in the front door just as Caroline came down the stairs. They met in the dining room at precisely the same time.

"Good morning," said Paula. Her lighthearted mood was a relief to the others, especially after last night's melancholy performance. "Why am I always so hungry up here at AngelFire? When I'm working in the city, I often forget to eat, but here my appetite is insatiable!"

"It's the mountain air and probably ten other things," answered Carmen. "We've got plenty of food, so please serve yourself."

"Thank you. I know it's not polite to eat and run, but I do have rehearsals today and I'll be leaving after breakfast. I'll have a long drive today and if I want to get back on time, I'll have to leave this morning."

Carmen asked her for more details about her little band and how many rooms they should get at the AngelFire Ski Lodge. Paula gave her all the particulars and Carmen went to her office to complete the reservations.

JB and Marti joined Paula, who was now on her second trip to the buffet, while Caroline poured herself a cup of coffee.

"Have you heard anything?" asked Carmen, softly.

"Not a peep."

Diana walked in praising the morning and looking radiant. "I think I slept on the moon last night! I woke up in the same position that I fell asleep and the bed barely looked slept in."

"I love hearing that from our guests," said Carmen "I hope it means you are feeling deep comfort."

"I am....this year. Anyone heard anything yet? I would like to call Jackson before he gets on that airplane tomorrow," said Diana. "Is anyone up for a hike after breakfast?"

"Well, actually.... we have a special day planned...," started Caroline, when Kate and Robbie, walked in together. The room became silent ...Caroline and Carmen held each other's hand.

Kate spoke first, "Before I begin, I want to apologize to all of you for some of the things I said last night. The dinner was superb and the gifts were incredibly thoughtful and truly beautiful."

Caroline and Carmen were not breathing. Together they lowered themselves onto a bench.

Robbie continued, "We know that our announcement last night gave you all reason to fly into a fury, yet each of you, especially JB for me...gave us nothing but your support. So Katie and I would like to thank all of you for the selfless kindness we've received. As you can imagine, we had a long night with a great deal to discuss..."

Kate interrupted, "And if you will forgive me for my outburst last night. I would like to say that the O'Neil – Collicci wedding is back on schedule."

Caroline and Carmen gave a sigh and a cheer along with the rest of their friends.

Marti was the first to hug Kate, "You nearly scarred me for life! You two are a match made in heaven. I was so confused!"

Robbie came to Caroline and whispered, "I thought I was going to lose her...I still don't understand completely, but at least I sealed the deal."

"My dear sweet Robbie, you will never understand Kate completely. That's marriage and that's life!" said Caroline. "I still say I will never completely understand Frank and well... never mind, we have happier things to deal with."

Sigrid made her way over to Robbie as he was getting his coffee and asked if he felt up to the quarterly review meeting.

"Sigrid? You look incredible! Katie didn't tell me - When did you – How did you – Who did you?" started Robbie. "I just don't know where to begin!" The normally articulate Robbie Collicci was nearly at a loss for words. "I'd be happy to meet with you this morning, Sigrid. I am just plain happy to do just about anything this morning," said Robbie.

"Thank you, Robbie."

"What did Arturo have to say when he saw you?" asked Robbie.

"He hasn't seen me yet, nor does he even know anything about it."

"Well then, this week is just full of surprises! I'd like to be present when he sees you, or at least close enough to see the look on his face," said Robbie with a wry grin.

"You'll be getting ready for the wedding, and what's going on between Arturo and me, will be the farthest thing from your mind.

I do have a few important questions to ask of you, so I hope we can all keep our feet on the ground for the meeting. I know how distracting love can be."

"Indeed, Ms. Kerrington, indeed."

"Great – so we can get together in Caroline's office after breakfast! She has other plans for Katie," said Sigrid.

The room was filled with anticipation for the upcoming wedding. Carmen caught a quiet moment and stood to make an announcement.

"Ladies...Caroline and I have a special day planned for all of you. Sorry JB and Robbie, your turn will have to come later." Carmen glanced over to Caroline, who nodded for her to continue. "Along with the renovations of the bungalows this year, we modernized our little Spa. Caroline has made arrangements for a full Spa Day for everyone. She has created a menu of spa services that you may choose from and you are guaranteed to be pampered. I suggest you choose them all!"

Caroline handed out the newly printed Spa Menus to each of her friends who were delighted with the prospects of a day of pampered luxury. Once the breakfasts were finished, each friend returned to her bungalow to retrieve her spa robe and slippers.

Kate stole away to an area for more privacy to say farewell, as Robbie was going to return to Santa Fe after his finance meeting with Sigrid. This would be the last time she would see him before the ceremony.

"Anything more you want to tell me before I leave?" he asked her, almost wishing he hadn't.

"I love you." She kissed him sweetly and then left the room to find Marti.

Caroline encouraged Carmen to join the others for the Spa Day explaining that she and Robbie were going to be meeting with Sigrid and would join them later. She expected the meeting to be a short one.

At 10:00 am Caroline returned to her office and cleared her desk. All papers regarding the wedding arrangements were placed in a file drawer in the credenza behind her desk. Robbie joined her first. He took a seat at the small round meeting table in the alcove of her office. The window overlooked the main entrance to the Inn and had a view of the bungalows. He was watching Kate and Marti walk toward the Spa.

"Have you spoken to my brothers?" asked Robbie.

"Yes, I have. I have to admit that having them here for the wedding is a little awkward for me after all these years," said Caroline.

"Katie has already met them, and I didn't want to keep them away from my wife. I know Frank regretted doing that, yet he never did anything about it. Katie thinks that they live in another world so far removed from hers, she will never understand them."

"I guess Frank thought his social worker wife wouldn't understand them either," said Caroline.

"Honestly, I think Frank was more worried that you *would* like them and that they would want to come to AngelFire, just a little too often," said Robbie.

Sigrid came into the office juggling a purple expanding file, a large purple binder, and her Spa Robe and slippers. "What are you two laughing about?"

"My brothers," said Robbie. "They're coming to the wedding."

"How much fun will that be? I haven't seen the *Blues Brothers* since Frank's service. Which one will be your Best Man?" asked Sigrid.

"I asked Giovanni," answered Robbie. "They will be arriving in Santa Fe tonight, and we'll all come to AngelFire together on Saturday afternoon."

"Sounds like a bachelor's party is in the works," said Sigrid.

"A dinner maybe," said Robbie. "I passed on a party."

"I'm guessing you're brothers don't take 'No' for an answer very easily," said Siggy. They are probably planning to take you out to some kind of wild *breastaurant* and try to get you drunk and you'll wake up back in Vegas!"

"Which is exactly why Frank kept them away from you, Caroline" said Robbie. "Enough about my zany brothers...Sigrid, do you have financials for me to review?"

Sigrid retrieved the documents from the expanding file and handed copies to Caroline and Robbie and held one for herself. "They are pretty much the same as the copies I sent to you by email. The numbers are similar to our last quarter, with the exception of some new expenditures under R & D."

"What are you looking into?" asked Robbie.

"Well, I know that our plan was to slowly build the business over a five year period and then decide if we're ready to sell, or extend development. I've been thinking about the whole Sara Lee model and wondering if it is worth the wait."

"What do you mean? You seemed so firm about it a year ago," said Caroline. "What has changed?"

"Sometimes when we have an idea, it needs a lot of tweaking before it works. Like all my old recipes, for instance...I haven't forgotten that. I had visions of grandeur with my name on every box. I've come to the conclusion that this was an ego-led dream. What I really wanted was financial security and freedom for my future. Running an operation the size of mine is a lot of work. Now that Arturo is running things smoothly, I think we can put the same effort into a larger operation, a little sooner. I know I am just about to celebrate my first anniversary, but he has twenty years in the commercial bakery industry and I've found a potential opportunity.

I've been talking to the RJ's markets, I brought them samples and they seemed to like our little pies – a lot! The hitch is that they want to do them under their name, instead of mine. They want to do both a twelve piece box and a twenty-four piece box, in the frozen desserts case.

"Do they want to test them regionally or go nationwide?" asked Robbie.

"They didn't use the word 'testing', they said they wanted to introduce them, region by region," answered Sigrid.

"What would stop a copycat from undercutting you by the end of the first year?" asked Caroline.

"There is probably a copycat out there right now, trying to copy 'Sigrid's Symphony Sweets', for all we know," said Sigrid. "I can't worry about that."

"Do you have any numbers on this?" asked Robbie.

Sigrid handed her big purple binder over to Robbie. Silently, he examined the documents.

"What does Arturo think about this?" asked Caroline.

"Since they have three hundred and sixty-five stores with more planned, he thinks we should seriously consider it, as long as we can try to get a five-year contract. We would have to add another shift and of course hire more people," said Sigrid.

"You are one ambitious blonde bombshell," said Robbie.

With jaw dropped, Caroline spoke first, "What are you saying, Robbie? Are you commenting on her idea or her appearance?"

"Well....I certainly don't mean to insult you, Sigrid. I think you're amazing! This is an opportunity that is going to require additional equipment, ingredients, supplies, time to train new employees, and greater cash outlays for all of it.

I know that you and Arturo must have discussed this thoroughly. I'd like to hear how much cash he thinks you will need," said Robbie.

"First of all, the truth is I can't do this without him, since he is the one with all the expertise. He is willing to run the night shift for the RJ's business and I can run the day shift for SS-Sweets. In order to make this work, I'll want to make him a partner," said Sigrid.

"Siggy, I really like Arturo, but won't that just complicate everything?" asked Caroline. "Won't this be a strain on your romantic relationship with him? What if we put more money into this and the two of you have a falling out and well...then what?"

"Wait, I wasn't very clear. We don't want you to put more money into this, he wants to *buy* into this business, build it together for five to ten years, and then if we still feel the same way about each other, we sell it, or a part of it, and create a nice life together.

He will be here on Saturday morning, along with a spectacular wedding cake, I might add. And Robbie, I know you won't be focusing on business, but you will get a chance to see us together. Although it has been less than a year since we've been dating and working together, I think you will see that Artie and I are a great team," answered Sigrid.

"I don't see any reason not to go forward. Let's get the *real* numbers and what kind of terms and contracts we can get lined up and see what happens. When Katie and I return from our honeymoon, we can sit down and figure out how to make this work," said Robbie. "It's happening fast, but you do have a great product and real potential here. We're just changing the model, that's all."

"What do you mean, changing the model?" asked Caroline. "We're not sticking to the Sara-Lee model?"

"I would call this the AngelFire Inn model," he answered.

Standing right behind her, stood a single specter of light in the outline of a man. He remained still; not visible to the others in the room. He leaned toward her and placed his arm of light around her and she *felt him*. Caroline was swept away with memories of conversations she'd had with Frank when they began their venture in AngelFire together... and she smiled.

Really, Caroline?

"Spas can become well-tended gardens where life-enhancing experiences are grown in harmony with nature's touch, tone and tempo."

Jonathan Paul De Vierville

Caroline and Sigrid were walking toward the Spa to join the others when Sigrid suddenly stopped and said, "I want to call Artie before it gets any later. Do you mind?"

"Of course not, I know you want to share the outcome of our meeting with him. Go ahead and just come over when you're ready."

"Have you told anyone about Artie?" asked Sigrid.

"Everyone knows you're seeing someone named Artie, from the bakery...and the rest is yours to tell," said Caroline with a broad smile. "Katie hasn't said anything, so I'm guessing that Robbie has never mentioned anything about him either."

"I don't think I'll have to say a word," said Sigrid.

"Well, I think everyone will be so focused on the new you, Artie will be taking a back seat! Anyway, say hello to him for me, and come join us at the Spa! "

When Caroline walked into the Spa, she reviewed the list of services for the day and the choices her friends had made. Carmen was in the sauna; Marti and Kate were in the massage treatment rooms; and Diana was about to get a pedicure. Caroline decided to join Diana and get a *mani-pedi* combination. She also signed up for a facial and the last massage of the day.

"Oh good!" said Diana. "Glad you could join me. How was your meeting?"

"Interesting...it seems our Ms. Sigrid may have changed her mind about becoming the *'Twenty-first Century Sara Lee'*, but I'll let her tell you about it – when she's ready. She still astounds me with her great dreams and schemes."

"I understand how it is when you have started something new and find out it's not all that you thought it might be," confessed Diana. "I love what I'm doing. I just don't know if I like all that comes with it. It's not enough to deliver a good message with hopes that you may inspire someone. There are eighty other things that also have to happen in your day and then, you still have to be a wife and mother."

"You're right, the *'Be-Do-And-Have-It-All'* refrains we used to hear encouraged a lot of women to move up and out into the world, but I don't remember anyone telling us how exhausting it would all become. At least in this chapter of our lives, our children are grown and we're not soccer moms anymore," said Caroline. "Are you considering making any changes?"

"No, not yet. I'm just praying about it. Jackson is incredibly passionate about his part of the ministry. I still think we're a good team in front of and behind the camera, so I'm not intending to disrupt anything. It's just that sometimes I feel like something is missing," said Diana.

"I know that feeling and I know what's missing for me, it's not *something* – *it's someone*. The truth is that AngelFire was Frank's dream, and it's not the same without him. My sister Julia was right. I will not be able to start a new life as long as I am here at AngelFire. It is so beautiful here and I have so much to be thankful for. What I do now affects many other people, so there's a lot to consider. "I guess I have a lot to pray about, too," said Caroline.

"*Really Caroline?* Frank's legacy has given you the gift of complete freedom. Go see the world for heaven's sake! No one would resent you for that. I'll bet they're all just waiting for you to just say 'Adios Amigos!' Take Julia –Take your sons–For that matter, take *me* with you!"

"Speaking of Julia, she'll be coming for the wedding, and my sons, will be here tomorrow afternoon.

Oh here's another wedding surprise...Ric called early this morning. He wants to come to the wedding! I told him he's welcome to join us and he can stay with one of the boys.

What time will the Greene girls be arriving...I've forgotten. I can't remember the last time I saw Lauren and Michelle. I know the boys will be glad to see them," said Caroline. "Maybe they can all share the ride coming up the mountain."

"Only if it will take all six of them – the girls timed their flights with their dad. Jackson plans to ride up here with them. Ric and Jackson and our babies, now there's a page from history," said Diana. "Except that in those days it would have been the church van, not a limousine! Does Kate have any idea that all our children will be attending this wedding?"

"She's known very little about this wedding and other than what we each told her last night, there are still quite a few surprises ahead for her. We don't want to rattle her any more than she already is, so let's not reveal any more to her when she comes out of that treatment room. Hopefully, the massage has relaxed her nerves. I wanted her to see all our families together, celebrating this beautiful occasion. I also want Robbie to know all of us as his family, too.

Marti's family will be here by Friday afternoon, too. Sigrid's boys can't make it and her daughter Sherri gave me a 'maybe' response, but I'm holding a room for her anyway."

"Sherri's the one who's in for a bit of a surprise when she sees her mother," said Diana.

"Not to mention her mother's *amoureux!*" said Caroline.

Diana and Caroline turned to see Carmen come out of the sauna wrapped in her terry robe with her hair wrapped in a towel. She gave a quick wave and went straight to the showers. Kate emerged from the treatment room and signaled *"a thumbs up"* toward Caroline as she made her way to the sauna. A few minutes later Marti appeared from the other treatment room and joined Caroline and Diana.

"I'm ready for a nap," said Marti. "There is nothing like an hour long massage to melt away all your stress. Katie and I also had lemon balm facials. This is all too delicious Caroline, and just what the doctor ordered for the bride. She is definitely more at ease today."

"Thanks Marti, that's exactly what I'd hoped to hear."

"So Marti, Caroline just told me your family is coming tomorrow afternoon, too. That's wonderful! I'll look forward to meeting Laney and seeing your sweet granddaughters. How is Erik, these days?"

"He is doing well, thank you. He just finished working on a project with his father, in Sweden. Amazing, isn't it? Erik and Erik seem to like each other a lot. It's me they are not too sure about. This has been quite an awkward time for all of us, in many ways. Erik Sr. and I are at least trying to be friends. After all these years, it has been hard for both of us to wrap our heads around our family situation. Not once have we spoken of the past - yet. The truth is we were just two kids in love, a very long time ago," said Marti.

"As I recall," said Caroline. "Those two kids were *very much* in love."

"Where is this going, Caroline?"

"Uh....he's single...and uh...you're *still* single, umm...."

"*Really Caroline*? Don't complicate things," said Marti

"WHY NOT?" said a chorus of her friends.

"Maybe it's time to start swimming at the deep end of the pool," said Caroline.

"Fear of drowning," responded Marti.

Just then, the front door opened and the perfect distraction materialized as two servers came in presenting a cart full of small salad dishes, a fruit tray, bowls of olives, and a platter of cheeses and tomato bruschetta. Two iced buckets were filled with sparkling waters and bottles of juices.

And just in time for lunch, Sigrid walked in beaming.

"Welcome, welcome!" said Marti. "Perfect timing, Siggy."

"Oh Good! Why is my timing so perfect?"

"Because now we can shift this conversation off of me and on to you," said Marti.

Carmen came round the corner glowing and vibrant. With a big smile she said, "I feel fantastic! And hungry, too."

"I think it's wonderful that you can participate in more of the retreat this year. We love your cooking Carmen, but we love your company even more," said Diana.

"What a kind thing for you to say, thank you! It looks like they've finished setting up for lunch. Is anyone ready to join me?" said Carmen.

"I will," said Sigrid, Marti and a voice shouting out from the shower room. Diana and Caroline were getting their toes polished and would join them within minutes. Katie appeared at the table in her spa robe like the rest of the women, with the exception of Caroline.

Six women sat around the table in their sage colored robes with the AngelFire insignia embroidered on the breast pocket in a merlot thread and recalled the last time they shared a meal in this attire. For a brief and silent moment, their thoughts went to the seventh friend, now missing. No one needed to say a word.

"Caroline, are you not staying with us this afternoon?" asked Kate, breaking the silence.

"Yes, I am. I booked a facial and massage in about an hour. I'll change my clothes, then."

"Siggy, how are you going to pamper yourself today? What services did you decide on?" Carmen asked.

"My doctor said I could have a selective massage, no facial, and I just had a manicure, so I think I will do a pedicure and fresh polish for my nails. I noticed some dazzling colors on the tray over there. What a great day! With this and what I've done in the past two weeks, I've had more self-pampering than I have since before I gave birth to my first child."

"Speaking of your children...did your daughter get a whole new gourmet kitchen after that fire last year?" asked Carmen.

"Yes she did, and every appliance, gadget and gizmo she could come up with is in it, too."

"Then I take it, that the two of you have made amends," said Kate.

"*Kinda-sorta*," said Sigrid. "Sherri seemed to think that since I am starting to make some real money, I should pay for part of this remodel, since the fire was my fault."

"What? What about her insurance? Didn't that pay for the new kitchen?" asked Kate.

"Of course it did, except that I'm guessing it didn't pay for all the extra bells and whistles she added onto the job," answered Sigrid.

"How did you work this out with her?" asked Diana.

"I told her that as soon as she reimbursed me for that college education for which I scrimped, saved and sacrificed – and which she never used – then we'd have something to talk about."

"Aaaaand so it is!" said Marti.

"Please pass the olives, Carmen," said Caroline, scrambling to change the subject, and making a mental note, that the room reserved for Sherri may be available tomorrow night after all.

"Let's toast the hosts!" said Marti. "I know this is just juice, but we're feeling awfully grateful to Caroline and Carmen, for this wonderful idea. Cheers!" There is nothing like a little statement of gratitude to shift the energy of the room, thought Marti.

"Katie, what will you do with your hair for the wedding?" asked Diana.

"Brush it," she answered, without hesitation.

"THAT'S IT?" said Carmen and Sigrid in unison.

"Wait a minute ladies, you are talking to a woman who wears vegan nail polish," said Marti.

"Can I help you with that?" asked Caroline and Diana, also in unison.

"The groom may not recognize her if you do," said Marti.

"We're helping you – this is your wedding day, for heaven's sake," said Caroline.

"Trust us, Katie. I promise you, when you look at your photo album a year from now, you will thank us. Caroline can put your hair up into something beautiful, and I'll do your make-up," added Diana.

"Make-up?"

"Dr. Woo-Woo, since we are all going to be glammed-up for your wedding, it seems appropriate for the bride to do the same. If I can do it, you can do it. We can't have Siggy stealing the show now, can we?" said Marti.

Who knows what?

*"The truth is you don't know what is going to happen tomorrow.
Life is a crazy ride, and nothing is guaranteed"*

Eminem

*F*or some inexplicable reason, Caroline was feeling anxious about the wedding plans. It was no small feat to coordinate flights from several destinations; ground transportation from Santa Fe to AngelFire; extra staff to accommodate a crowded Inn; the wedding service, the reception dinner, the bar, a photographer, flowers, cake, the entertainment and additional meals and activities for the next few days, all under the direction of the bride and groom who said to "just keep it simple".

It was certainly not a large wedding, for it was just "family". Not blood relatives, but a family of choice, deeply bonded by their history, sorrows and triumphs. Each had been a shoulder for the other when needed, especially in the past few years, with the loss of Frank and Nicole. They were elated to come together for a more joyous occasion, such as this. Spouses and children would only make this gathering even more memorable.

Caroline checked and rechecked the airline flights. She hesitated calling Carmen for support, for she had her own long checklist. *Thank God for JB*, she thought. He had such a good rapport with all the staff that she was confident they would perform beautifully.

Her thoughts turned toward the Amoroso brothers. She had only met them twice and really knew almost nothing about them. She was clearly in a stupor when she last saw them, at Frank's funeral. They arrived in a limousine, came in black Armani suits, never removed their sunglasses, stayed in the background, and left early with Robbie. Would they bring dates? Robbie had referred to them as his "zany brothers". Does that mean they would bring showgirls? Blackjack dealers? Wild women or tame? *Who knows what they might do,* she thought.

Then she felt that sensation on her shoulder again.

Her cell phone rang and she flinched. To her surprise, it was Robbie.

"Robbie? Is everything all right?" asked Caroline.

"Of course, why? Is there something wrong up there?" asked Robbie.

"No, I'm just a little anxious tonight. Everything went well today, but who knows what tomorrow will bring," answered Caroline.

"I don't know about tomorrow, but I do know that two – not three – of my brothers will be coming to AngelFire with me on Saturday. Sal will have to stay in Las Vegas for business reasons, so I will it just be Giovanni and Antonio. And I told them – no girlfriends. I thought I'd call just in case you were worried. We'll stop in Taos, so don't plan on us for lunch, okay?"

"I wasn't worried, really. I just want everything to be perfect," she said.

"I do too, Caroline. I do too."

Following their goodbyes, Caroline glanced around the room, then looked up and said, *"Thanks, Frank."*

The Way We Were

We all have our time machines. Some take us back, they're called memories. Some take us forward, they're called dreams.

- Jeremy Irons

*A*s Caroline descended the back stairs, she heard laughter, loud hearty laughter, coming from the dining room. She served herself a glass of wine in the butler's pantry and joined her friends at the dining table. Her friends had finished their dinner and were enjoying cappuccinos. "What is so hilarious?"

"We're going through the photo album and scrapbook that Marti and Erik made for Katie," said Carmen. "We just found a picture of you that looks like it was taken in the late '70's with your huge hair, false eyelashes and go-go-boots."

"It looks like Cleopatra did your make-up," said Marti.

"Let me see that," said Caroline. "Look at the hot pink mini-dress! Well, I'm sure not twenty-four anymore! All right then, did Erik also put in a photo of his mother from that decade?" she

145

asked as she flipped through the pages. "Look - here's Angela Davis! No, I beg your pardon, it's Martha Westerlund. Look at that Afro – it's massive!"

And after another round of laughter, Marti took the book and found another great photo, "Check this one out," she said as she passed the book on. It was a girl with long, curly red hair, big round glasses and a scarf banded across her head and tied over her left ear. She wore bell bottoms, a long sweater and no make-up.

"Awwww Katie, what a sweet little hippie you made," said Diana. The photo showed Kate holding baby Erik.

"Thank you, Diana. I'm glad you saw this," said Kate. "I have always preferred the natural look. So please keep this in mind when you to try to do something with my face before my wedding."

"We'll only make you more beautiful," said Caroline.

"Just make sure Robbie will be able to identify the bride," said Kate.

Marti took the book again and found a photo of Sigrid. She slid the book over to Diana and said, "Who do you think that is?"

"Doris Day? Donna Reed? Mrs. Cleaver?" asked Diana. "Well?"

"Don't be so shocked – that was me!" said Sigrid. "I tried to be like all three of those women. Even in the '70's and '80's, while you three were figuring out how to break glass ceilings."

"Siggy, we didn't break any glass ceilings. Not one of us. We're all doing a little of that now at this stage of our lives. In those days, I was still following my husband around the country and trying to pick up a part time job as a social worker," said Caroline.

"And I was playing the organ for churches, like the one where we met," said Marti.

"And I was a nurse. I hadn't entered the world of Chinese or holistic medicine yet," said Kate.

"Look at this photo, Siggy," said Caroline. "Here's Brad's first day at Mrs. Kerrington's Day Care. Looks like I lost Cleopatra's telephone number. And look at that awful green polyester pantsuit! And my hair is in a ponytail! I wonder if I even looked into a mirror that day."

"Okay, Carmen and Diana, this is not fair that we don't have pictures of your past," said Sigrid.

"I'll bet I do," said Caroline. "But I'm sure there's not even one that will make you laugh."

"Cry maybe, but definitely not laugh," said Carmen. "I was in school then, wearing jeans and a t-shirt every day, all the way through graduation. JB and I both had big ponytails, only he is still wearing his. I have been trying to get him to cut it off for the past year, and he won't even consider it. He'd be happy if he could wear the same old jeans and t-shirts, too."

"Do you think he will ever give up the ponytail?" asked Marti.

"He'll probably be buried in it," said Carmen

"Here's a photo I don't remember ever seeing before," Caroline said. "It's all three of us with our kids. There's Erik, Sherri, and Jarrod. Siggy, you *do* look like Doris Day! Katie you have that same scarf around your head and....hey, wait a minute...Is this some of Erik's magic?"

"Yes, I confess...I wasn't going to say a word, unless one of you noticed it. Erik's a master at Photoshop. He can make us look older, younger, thinner, huge, change our hair color – you name it! He edited four different photos to get us together in that single frame. He didn't have a photo that would work for Siggy's boys or your son Brad."

"Well I love the album and I think I will hire Erik to edit boxes full of my photos," said Kate.

" Marti, I would love to have a copy of that photo," said Caroline.

"So would I, please," said Sigrid.

You know, as we look at all of these old photos, it reminds me of just how long we've had each other to lean on," said Caroline. That last picture we're all talking about was taken when I had returned to California, going through a separation from Ric. Brad was probably at school, Siggy had Jarrod; and I was looking for a job. Not a favorite time in my life, but I always had all of you just a phone call away."

"Not me," said Carmen.

"You –I call on every day - now! While I was upstairs, I realized that we have been through divorces and deaths together, babies and business, together – but for the first time, we're all together for a wedding! How great is that?"

"So what is it like to be a wife?" asked Kate.

"I have no idea," answered Marti.

"And I have forgotten," said Sigrid.

"My husband and I are like a compass for each other. We hope to inspire each other to be our best selves. He is my rock, especially when I occasionally get lost - mostly in unimportant details," said Diana.

"JB and I grew up in the same place, but we're often two very different people. He is such a creature of habit, always responsible and a very quiet man. I think together, we are a rock for other people," offered Carmen.

"There are no predetermined roles anymore," said Caroline. "Marriage has been given a clean slate. I think that with Ric, I was always so impressed by his need to see that '*The Right Thing*' was always done in his public life, by his associates, his friends, and of course, our family. That's why he was so devastated when I left him. He could not fathom that divorce was the right action for our circumstances. Look at the whole Roberts family, Katie. They are all activists on one level or another.

Being a wife to Frank was very different. We led a very private life, incredibly romantic and nurturing. I was enormously happy. But my husband had many secrets, and I was willing to make the trade-off...to just look away, not ask too many questions, and trust him completely. How real was it – I can't answer that question, and honestly, I don't think I would do it any differently.

So my dear Katie, you will create a marriage based on your own needs and desires. You're at a very different stage in life and you'll have to decide on the "happily-ever-after" based on your love for him and your personal needs and desires. You will have to work at it, just like everyone else. And – you have all of us to call, anytime you want to share your joy or your sorrow along the way. We all get both."

"Amen," said the married and formerly married women around the table.

Thank God it's Friday!

"And thank you for a house full of people I love. Amen."

~Terri Guillemets

"Robbie? Is everything all right?" asked Caroline, completely caught off guard by the early morning call from the bridegroom, the day before the wedding.

"Fine – I'm fine. Listen, I have a request. I just called JB and asked him to join me and my brothers for a night on the town. He can stay here at my place tonight and return to AngelFire with us tomorrow."

"Well...what did he say?" she wondered.

"He said he's never left you alone on an *'incoming'* weekend. What do you think? Do you need him?"

"We do have a lot going on today, but I think we can handle it. What made you decide to invite him now?" she asked.

"Truth?"

"Of course!"

"My brothers have some kind of plan set up for me and I want a safe, sane and sober JB, to come along and protect me from their antics, just in case it gets a little too crazy."

"Seriously?"

"There will be nothing serious about this little party," answered Robbie. "Don't worry – we'll all be there on time tomorrow afternoon."

"I've gotta go, my other line is ringing. Have fun!"

"Thanks, Caroline. I didn't want this to be a problem for you," said Robbie.

⚜

"Good morning JB!" Caroline said cheerfully. "He did? Carmen's okay with it, too? Great! Hey, don't worry about us. The staff is completely reliable and we'll call you if we have any problems or questions. Go! Just have some fun for a change."

⚜

And once more...the phone rang...

"Carmen? Of course it's okay. When is the last time your husband went out without you?

Oh...."

⚜

Caroline went down to the kitchen and made some coffee. She'd been up for a while enjoying the last few minutes of the stillness of the morning. She heard the back entrance door open and thought it might be someone from the kitchen staff coming in to prepare breakfast. Instead, it was a dour-faced Carmen.

"By that look on your face I can't tell if you are worried or angry, or - are you jealous?" said Caroline. She put an arm firmly around Carmen's shoulder and said, "I'm sure it will be fine today. We can handle this."

"Do you have any idea how hard it is for me to get my husband to take me out for anything special? And on this particular weekend with so much to do..."

"Carmen, your face is turning green. You know very well that if we had planned something special for Katie today, that JB would have encouraged you to go and have a good time. We have a lot of extra help today; we will manage this – you and I – very well. I promise – we'll be so busy we won't even notice he's gone."

"I'll notice when he doesn't come home tonight," she said with a pouting face. "Okay... I get it. I just needed to vent for a minute. He'll be back tomorrow in time to get out of his jeans and into the new suit I bought him for the wedding. He doesn't know I bought it yet, but it will be too late to argue about it."

"All right then, before the breakfast team arrives, I want to get back upstairs and get myself ready for the day. Only you and I know all those who will be attending this wedding. Robbie has no idea how many will be here, and I guess Katie will figure it all out by dinner. Do we have the larger dining room tonight at Stonewood? I have a feeling we should prepare for extras, just in case," said Caroline.

"Who would bring extra people to a private wedding?" asked Carmen.

"My sons...they are coming in with their father."

"JB told me that he was very kind and considerate of you at the hospital on the night of Nicole's accident," said Carmen. "He also said that you two seemed very comfortable together."

"Did he also tell you that Ric had a cell phone in his ear and he was texting on another one at the same time?"

"He mentioned it," answered Carmen.

"I've got to go upstairs and dress for the day. Even though we think we've covered everything, I have this uncanny feeling that you and I are in for a few surprises. *Good ones- I think*!" she said, and she climbed the stairs up to her apartment.

We hope, thought Carmen.

At breakfast Caroline, Diana, Carmen, Marti and Sigrid were chatting about the arrival of their families. Caroline announced the impending arrival of her ex-husband, Ric. Diana confirmed that both her daughters would also be coming with their father, Jackson. Marti prepared the group for the barrage of baby items that no doubt her son Erik, and daughter-in-law, Laney, would have packed into their minivan and would bring all the way up the mountain. Sigrid was still uncertain about Sherri's attendance, but thrilled that Arturo would be her escort for the evening.

"I can't wait for you to meet him," she said with a smile.

The room went silent as Kate entered.

"What?" she asked, as she stood standing with her hands on her hips.

"*Nothing*" they answered, with some hesitation.

"How's the bride this morning?" asked Caroline. "Come to the table and join us! We're just excited about the wedding, that's all."

Diana asked Kate, "Would you like to take a hike with me up to the lake after breakfast? I thought maybe we could use some exercise and take in some of the gorgeous colors Mother Nature has started to provide for us."

"What a great idea!" Caroline, Diana and Marti chimed in.

"Sounds like you are trying to get me away from here for a couple of hours, which truthfully, sounds good to me," answered Kate.

"Maybe I should take you out for a trip to Santa Fe to spy on the groom's bachelor party," said Carmen. "Did you know my husband is on his way to join them?"

"No I didn't, and since you've told me that, I won't be too worried about them. The Amoroso brothers are just free birds. I've met them all twice this year and they seemed harmless. They're all quite good looking, and they live in a world of their own creation," said Kate.

"Isn't that a nice way of saying they live by their own rules?" asked Marti.

"Since both Frank and Robbie chose to keep their distance from them, yet stayed in contact, I'm presuming that they're just unconventional men, not gangsters," answered Kate.

"You are not making me feel any better about this little party," said Carmen.

"Oh, stop – look who we're talking about. JB? Robbie? These are reasonable, bright men," said Diana.

"And would you want Jackson to go 'out on the town' with them tonight?" asked Carmen.

"Not on your life! Some photographer would catch him in an odd moment, and he might lose everything we've worked for," answered Diana.

"Okay, this has all been very interesting, but I have a staff to meet with this morning. Diana and Katie, enjoy your walk. Carmen, you should come with me, in case the staff have any questions I can't answer," said Caroline.

"Siggy and Marti, do you want to join us for a long walk?" asked Kate.

"Um...no thank you, I want to just relax today," said Sigrid, looking rather guilty.

"Me too," added Marti, without any guilt.

⚜

From the beginning, JB was every bit the manager that Frank had told Caroline he would be. Each staff member knew exactly what and how to do their job. They had never had a day without JB to support them but were obviously up to the tasks at hand. Over half their guests would arrive by Friday afternoon, with the remaining guests due by noon, on Saturday.

Paula and her band would arrive Saturday afternoon. She relinquished Miss Cheyenne's bungalow to stay with her teen band members at the ski lodge. Camille MacArthur, the cellist, and friend of Paula's, agreed to act as an additional chaperone for the teens.

By noon, all rooms and bungalows were ready. Roberto Niccolini and the kitchen staff had arrived to receive and prep some of the provisions for the wedding dinner. The housekeeping staff had made the Inn sparkle for Caroline, knowing how much this weekend meant to her. The last time many of these people had gathered together was for Frank Amoroso's funeral. This occasion would be centered on the love of the bride and groom and the joys of friendship.

At 2:00 pm, a limousine came slowly up the long AngelFire Inn's drive. It stopped directly in front of the entrance, where Caroline and Diana were standing, waiting for the passengers. The driver opened both sides of it and the laughter was heard before the faces of Caroline's sons, and Diana's daughters were seen. Jackson emerged first, helping his daughters out of the car. The ballerina and the attorney could not have been more different from each other. Lauren, the ballerina, ran to fully embrace her mother. Michelle, still in a business suit, dutifully joined them. The four Greenes held a loving moment together.

"Mom!" said Jarrod and Brad as they clasped their arms around Caroline. Ric, joined them as he would have at another time in their lives. These were the people he had loved the most. "You look beautiful," Ric said to Caroline handing her a bouquet of white roses. "These used to be a favorite of yours. Thank you for including me this weekend."

The Greenes and the Roberts had not been together as families in many years and the warmth between them was palpable. Caroline led them into the Inn, and reintroduced everyone to Carmen, who gave each of them keys to their rooms, directions, and a schedule.

Caroline's sons, along with their dad, went up to the second floor to find their rooms and to freshen up before dinner. The Greene girls followed them, while Diana took Jackson over to settle in to the Prairie Rose bungalow. All agreed to meet at 5:30 pm for drinks and hors d' oeuvres before they boarded the vans for dinner elsewhere.

Carmen approached Caroline with a wry little smile, and said, "Your boys get more handsome every year. It was very sweet of Ric to bring you those flowers."

"It was. It is nice to see him with the boys, but a little awkward for me, here at AngelFire," said Caroline.

"No time for uncomfortable feelings this weekend," said Carmen. "If I have to be comfortable with my husband being *'God knows where'* tonight, you have to be comfortable with your ex-husband here to attend your friend's wedding. Just be glad he doesn't have another wife or girlfriend for you to deal with."

"He wouldn't be here if he had either one," said Caroline.

"He didn't have a cellphone in his ear and wasn't texting anyone either," noted Carmen.

"Okay – we're even."

⚜

At 4:00 pm, Caroline was in her apartment, laying out her clothes for the evening when she noticed another car approaching. There was only one couple that drove a white Mercedes and was due at this wedding. She hurried downstairs to meet them in the foyer.

"Julia! David! I'm so glad you made it safely," said Caroline. "I thought you were coming tomorrow!"

"Caroline, you're looking like your old self again," said David as he embraced her.

"Her young self, David" said Julia. "We don't use the "o" word anymore, remember?"

"I'll take that as a compliment anyway, David," said Caroline as she leaned over to hug her sister, too. "I'm so glad you're here."

"Have Brad and Jarrod arrived yet?" asked Julia.

"Yes, they have, and you will see them at dinner. You may want to get settled into your bungalow and get ready for dinner. We are all meeting in the great room for drinks at 5:30 pm. You will be joining us, won't you?"

"Of course we will," said David. "Julia, I'll get the bags. Which bungalow are we staying in?"

"I'll walk you over there. You're staying in Bungalow number five, 'Miss Cheyenne'. They've all been recently redecorated. Everyone seems to be enjoying the new designs."

Caroline walked arm and arm with her sister over to the bungalow. She opened the bungalow and let Julia and David enter before her.

"*Yeehaw, this is some mighty fine digs y'all got here*," said David. "*Dang! This here paintin' over the fireplace is mighty nice, Miss Caroline. I take it this here's Miss Cheyenne.*"

"My husband sounds like he's watched too many Bonanza reruns," said Julia. "Really dear, this is quite lovely and it has great character. You still have the touch, Caroline. I hope I have the opportunity to see the other bungalows before we leave."

"I'm so glad you like it. Now you two relax a bit and I'll see you in the great room, at five thirty-ish."

As Caroline was walking back toward the Inn, she met with Marti. "Have you seen Katie or Siggy?"

"Yes, they came back from a walk about forty five minutes ago; they're in their bungalows resting before dinner. Perfect – huh?" Marti started waving at an incoming minivan. "Oh good - They're here!" The van looked jam-packed.

Carmen came out the front entrance and joined Caroline and Marti, to welcome them. "I paged two staff members; they can help with the luggage and baby bags, and stuff."

"Oh you just missed Julia and David. I took them over to Miss Cheyenne. Where were you?" asked Caroline.

"I was checking out the kitchen. They're doing some amazing work in there!" said Carmen.

"You were checking out the kitchen or the chef?" teased Marti.

Carmen ignored her and said, "I'm so happy your family could make it. I haven't seen your little granddaughters before. This is exciting!"

"The four-year old, Lilly, will be our flower girl tomorrow evening," said Marti proudly.

The minivan made it as close to the entry as possible and as Erik opened the door, he walked straight to his mom and embraced her. "I hope it's okay that we brought all this baby stuff...you know how Laney is," he whispered.

One of the staff members opened the door for Laney, while another opened a side sliding door to start retrieving the barrage of baby items, when out of nowhere appeared a six foot tall, blond haired, blue-eyed man that four year old Lilly, was calling 'Papa'.

"Erik?" said Caroline and Marti in unison.

"Welcome to the AngelFire Inn," said Carmen.

"I hope this is okay," said Erik Sr.

"I wanted my dad to meet my whole family," said Erik, Jr. "And since we're rarely all together, I thought this would be the perfect time."

"Perfect," said Marti, while trying to retain her composure.

"No problem, we have a room for you," said Carmen.

"We do?" whispered Caroline.

"Let's let our staff bring all your things in and I'll give you each your room keys," said Carmen.

"Perfect," said Marti, again.

Carmen gave keys to adjoining rooms to Laney. One was for her and Erik and the second room was complete with a full size crib for baby Lisa and a double bed for her big sister Lilly, and both opened up nicely for a full view of each other.

Carmen gave a third key to Erik Sr. for the room across the hall. She gave all of them instructions for the pre-dinner gathering and the dinner. Laney insisted that Erik drive her and the girls over in their own minivan due to the car seats situation. Caroline and Carmen were relieved of one more detail. When all were in their rooms, Marti, Caroline and Carmen returned to the foyer, without saying a word.

"Are you okay with this?" Caroline asked Marti. "Maybe you two should sit with Ric and me tomorrow at the reception, so we can all feel awkward together."

"This is not an accident," said Carmen. "You have been brought together for a reason, and during an evening that will be a celebration of love. I cannot think of a more graceful way to come together."

"Riiiiiight..." answered the two women.

Truth Be Told?

"The truth is rarely pure and never simple."

- Oscar Wilde

Caroline's cell phone was buzzing - again. It was Ric, - again.

"Can I speak with you for a minute, somewhere privately?"

"Absolutely, I'm in my apartment on the floor above you. It's open, come on up," she said, confident that he wanted to diffuse any uneasiness between them before the wedding. Ric had always been a direct communicator. He had enough secrets in his line of work, whatever that was.

"Sorry to bother you on such a busy day," Ric said as he walked into her apartment. "Well, this is an attractive place. I'll bet you find solace up here and just let the world go by."

"Not the entire world," answered Caroline. "The apartment is very private and visually such a departure from the rest of the Inn, it gives me a feeling of separateness." She invited Ric to sit in one of a pair of large overstuffed club chairs and then sat directly across from him. "Can I get you anything?"

"No thank you. You seem pretty isolated up here in these mountains. Is that what you want for your life now?" he asked.

"Oh, we keep pretty busy. Our rooms are booked several months ahead, so as I see it, the world comes to us. But you're right; more often lately, I do feel isolated. I did some traveling with Julia this year, which was a nice re-entry to the land of the living. Was there something else, Ric?" she asked.

"Yes, I want to tell you what's happened in Nicole's accident case. The blue truck was found – It had been repaired, painted another color and sold. The original owners had a teenage son, who happened to go to the school where Nicole had been teaching. The entire family had left town, and left no forwarding address. We finally tracked them down to a small town in Rhode Island. There were two other female students whose families also left town, quickly and without explanation. We found one in the Chicago area and the other outside of Atlanta. They haven't been questioned, yet. We think there was a second male. We don't know for sure, but we'll find out, soon. It's not clear if these kids caused the accident or not. Of course, no charges have been filed yet. I'm thinking this will still take some more time. It's a bit difficult, since they all are in different states.

"How badly do you want all the answers," asked Caroline.

"I think we owe it to Niki to get to the truth," said Ric.

"Do Lila or the boys know anything yet?" asked Caroline.

"Only that there is an ongoing investigation;"

"Then let's keep it that way until we know more; Paula is still pretty fragile yet, too. What do you think? Should we wait it out or tell them?" she asked.

"It could be a few more weeks or a few more months. I think we can wait a little longer, too. My best guess is that these kids know exactly what happened," he said.

"Do you have their names?"

"Yes, and I have the driver of the truck....his name was Paul Davies."

"Oh, God," she cried as her eyes welled up. *"The scream.* She screamed 'Paul' at the end."

"I know," he said, as he leaned forward to reach out to her. "I'm sorry, I wanted to tell you after the wedding, but I thought it would be worse. After this wedding everyone will leave happy and full of hope. I didn't want to ruin that. We should let it last as long as possible."

"Right – thank you, Ric. We can deal with this when there is something more concrete."

"I guess...I'll go, then. I'll see you downstairs for drinks, later. By the way, I'm staying with Brad. If you need me for anything, just call me in the room or on Brad's cell."

"Where's your cell phone?" she asked.

"For this weekend – it's in a drawer, at home."

"On purpose?"

"Yes, on purpose..."

The Family We Chose

"Call it a clan, call it a network, call it a tribe, call it a family. Whatever you call it, whoever you are, you need one."

~Jane Howard

*A*t five-thirty, nearly all members of the AngelFire clan had arrived in the great room and were enjoying wine and hors d'ouevres. Marti had stayed behind and purposely delayed Kate, until she got a signal from Caroline to bring her over. All the attention was focused on Erik's sweet little girls in their matching pink frilly dresses – until the moment came when Marti brought in the unsuspecting bride.

"SURPRISE!" shouted everyone, and the tears began to roll. Hugs and kisses and heartfelt wishes went round the room. Kate was overwhelmed and virtually speechless.

"A toast to the bride!" said Ric, and all held their glasses high, and cheered.

"Ric Roberts?" said Julia, from across the room. She pulled her husband David over toward the familiar voice.

"Julia – David, how nice to see you," he said, while shaking David's hand.

"Caroline said there would be some surprises, but I thought they'd all be for Kate. How are you? Are you still in the FBI or CIA or Secret Service or whatever it is that you do?" said Julia.

"Yes."

"Yes – what? Which one is it?" David asked.

"Yes – and that's all I can tell you," he answered.

"You know David, Ric's our American version of James Bond," said Julia.

"You always had quite an imagination Julia," replied Ric. "Have you seen the boys?"

"We have; they look great and we're told they are doing very well."

"Have you met Erik?" asked Julia.

"Erik or 'THE Erik'?" answered Ric.

"What the heck are you talking about?" said David.

"I'll tell you later dear. It is a very, very old story," said Julia.

"Have you met the groom, Robbie?" said Julia.

"No, I haven't. I'd like to meet the guy who stole Katie's heart," answered Ric.

"Well then, where is he?" asked David.

"Apparently having a Bachelor's Party and he has JB with him!"

"By tomorrow night, we'll all know each other very well, I'm sure," said Ric. "If you will excuse me, I'd like to go and congratulate the bride."

"Wait Ric – who's the blonde standing by Marti?" asked David.

"Sigrid – she looks remarkably well, doesn't she?" said Ric.

"Amazing! David, be a dear and get me another drink – I'll be right back," said Julia as she made a beeline directly toward Sigrid.

Ric found Kate and asked, "May I give you a very long and overdue hug? I am utterly thrilled for you, Katie."

"Ric Roberts, I'm so glad you are here! Thank you so much for coming. I think the whole family is here, now. I can't believe that

Caroline was able to pull this off! I wish Robbie were here so you could meet him tonight," said Kate.

"I'll look forward to meeting him at the wedding. Have you already spoken to Brad and Jarrod?" he asked.

"I have and I can't get over how much Brad looks like you. You must be so proud of them both. It looks like Jarrod is on his way over here with Michelle Greene. They're not kids anymore, are they Ric?"

"No they're not, and sometimes it makes me feel very old," admitted Ric.

Carmen and Caroline were beginning to herd the crowd into the vans for the drive to Stonewood. Caroline approached Ric; she leaned into him and whispered, "Go get Erik and Marti and ask them to sit with us."

"Are we sitting together? Uh-Good!" said Ric, thinking he would be sitting with his sons. "I'll go and look for them."

Stonewood had set up a private dining room with a bar and a round table for eight, which the younger generation seized immediately. A rectangular table for twelve served to accommodate their parents, a.k.a. aunts, and uncles.

"This is quite a beautiful family you raised our son to be a part of," said Erik, Sr., leaning over to Marti.

"Yes they are; we're a family of choice. Erik considers the group at that table his cousins, and each of these women has been a big part of his life," said Marti. "Ric and the Roberts family always included Erik in their family events, too. I'm sorry you never met his sister Nicole, she was the boys' chauffeur until they all went to college."

"Yes I know. Erik has told me a great deal about his childhood. He says he grew up surrounded by people who loved and supported him. You did a great job, Marti."

"We were lucky...blessed is more like it....and it all started with Caroline." Tears welled in a wistful memory. Erik placed his hand over hers and gave it a squeeze.

And at the other end of the table.....

"I can't believe I'm sitting at this dinner alone...without my husband," said Carmen. sitting next to Katie, who sat at the end.

"I can't believe this is my last night to be at one of these parties alone...I can hardly believe it. Tomorrow I will have a *husband*," said the bride-to-be.

"I can't believe that I won't be coming alone and will actually be bringing *a date* to your wedding tomorrow!" said Sigrid. "I think this calls for a toast to the three of us. Tomorrow everything will be different. Katie will be married and will start a new life; JB will return and you'll go back to your normal life; and Artie will be here, and God only knows what this will mean in my life."

And from the middle of the table....

Jackson Greene leaned forward and said, "It seems like yesterday our children were telling us they didn't want a "kid's table" anymore."

"Yes, and they seem very happy to be all together again," added Diana.

"Erik seems to be talking business with your sons, Caroline. I can tell by the way he tilts his head and leans forward," said Marti. "I have no idea what it could be, do you?"

"I'm afraid I'm clueless on this one," said Caroline. "They're probably talking football."

"I think I know what they're cooking up over there, but they need to speak with their mother, first," said Ric. "If I'm right, they'll speak with you after the wedding."

"Good, because I don't want to have to think about another thing until after our Katie gets married!"

"Julia, are you and David enjoying your retirement?" asked Diana.

"Are we retired?" asked David.

"Well, we're not, really," said Julia. "David and I have immersed ourselves in a project for the unemployed and homeless. We've had a good life and are grateful for all we have. So many people have lost their jobs, or lost their homes, and we wanted to do something besides play more golf. So we volunteer at – HFA – Homeless Families Assistance."

"It started out to be one day a week and now we're there three days a week," added David.

"What exactly do you do?" asked Carmen.

"The center offers food distribution, clothing distribution, and job counseling. Several social workers are available to evaluate individuals for other social services. We even have a little child care center for welfare moms," said Julia. "David has actually helped many of the men find jobs. He makes sure they have an 'interview suit' and if they don't have a car, he will drive them to an interview."

"Well that's impressive," said Sigrid.

"Don't get too impressed – we still play golf and we still travel, but we find a lot of fulfillment in our work," added Julia.

"And my friends, my sister Julia has lived her whole life like that, and she was the very reason I became a social worker," said Caroline.

"Let's have a toast to all the good women at this table who have lived their lives in service to others," said Jackson. "Let's have our children join us on this one, too." And if synchronized wine toasting were a sport, this group would have won a medal.

As the dinners were finished, the sons and daughters of the women of AngelFire, pulled their chairs over to their parent's table and mingled with their chosen aunts and uncles.

Erik leaned over to Ric and whispered confidentially, "It appears that I have missed out on a wonderful family."

"And for the most part, so did I – so did I," said Ric.

Caroline and Carmen organized the vans for the return trip to the Inn. After all the laughter, good food and good wine, and all guests returned to their rooms or bungalows, or wherever they went, the two of them sat alone with their feet up on an ottoman, in front of the glowing embers of a dying fire in the great room.

"Did we miss anything for tomorrow, Carmen? Did you wake up in the middle of the night remembering anything I may have forgotten?" asked Caroline. "I don't think I want any more surprises."

"No, I think we have everything covered. I think we can sleep well tonight. This was an easy, smooth night, don't you think? Everything went as planned," said Carmen. "Not perfect, but a great night."

"I know what you're thinking," said Caroline. "You missed having your husband here tonight."

"I did; I missed not having him sit next to me at dinner, and I missed how helpful he is when we have these events. I'll miss him even more tonight," admitted Carmen.

"I missed him, too. I missed Frank tonight, again. I wonder if I will ever stop missing him."

"Probably not," answered Carmen. "Sometimes, I still think he is here. Not so much anymore, but sometimes..."

Across the room, behind them both, stood a specter of light in the shape of a man, soundless and still....present, yet imperceptible...

Breakfast for 20...

"I need breakfast! If I were any more hungry right now, Brad and Angelina would adopt me..."

Anonymous

Caroline met Carmen at the coffee pot at sunrise and both were a bit bleary-eyed. "Were you able to sleep?" she asked.

"Not very well," said Carmen.

"Did you speak to JB?" she asked.

"He called, but there was so much noise in the background I could barely understand a word he said. He said something about a size, a bling, the king, a thing – it was just too hard to tell," said Carmen. "He also sounded like he was laughing – a lot! My serious husband was laughing and having a good time – wherever it was that they were."

"Well, at least he called. We had a great time last night, too," said Caroline. "The breakfast team should be here soon, and I want to get prepared for the day, so I'll meet you back here at eight-thirty, okay?"

"I'll focus on the breakfast, you focus on the chapel," said Carmen. "The delivery trucks are supposed to arrive at eight. The florist's crews should be here by ten-thirty. I hope that gives them enough time.

"Eight – right, then, I'll be back before eight. I'm sure Robbie and his brothers will have JB back here by noon, don't you think?"

"I hope so," said Carmen.

"This will be an interesting breakfast crowd. How many did you set for?" asked Caroline.

"We're preparing for twenty-four – just in case someone else shows up that we hadn't planned on."

"I really would love to sit with everyone, but I can only stay for a short time. I would like to eat breakfast with my sons, before I get too busy."

"And –their father. He is a good man, Caroline."

Caroline ignored her comment and headed up the stairs, to prepare herself for the excitement of the day.

❦

Julia and David were the first to arrive in the dining room, and Carmen was there to greet them. Carmen joined them for coffee and a little pastry, as the staff began to set out the breakfast buffet.

"So much has changed up here in just a year," said Julia. "It's good to see Caroline so engaged in her work. She looks happy and healthy and seems to be enjoying herself again."

"Yes, she's had a lot of creative projects this year to keep her mind moving in a forward direction. This wedding has summoned all her artistry, too. It's been a lot of hard work but you're right – it's been a very good year. Robbie has really stepped in for Frank and we could not have done all this without his guidance."

"That's what Caroline said, too. I still don't understand why Frank kept so many secrets."

"Well that's all over now and we've got a wonderful wedding planned – even without Robbie's guidance. It will be interesting to see his reaction."

"When do I get to meet the groom?" asked David.

"We're expecting them about noon," said Carmen.

Marti, Sigrid and Kate arrived in the dining room, and about the same time Ric and Erik came down the stairs together. Two by two, the Greene girls, and the Roberts boys also arrived. Laney and Erik came downstairs with the little ones, shortly after. Carmen greeted each one of the family guests and led them to the sumptuous breakfast buffet and asked them to select their own tables. She asked them to *"mix-it-up-a-little"* and also offered to sit with Lilly and baby Lisa, so Erik and his wife could visit with the rest of their friends and family. Carmen did just fine with the little ones and had them both giggling within minutes. Eventually, Marti came to the table to help her out. The girls were glad to see their grandmother, and Carmen was glad for a little assistance.

"Marti, why don't you take one of the girls over to see their grandpa," said Carmen

"Why?" asked Marti.

"Why not?" said Carmen.

Then Lilly expressed her opinion and shouted, "Papa, papa, papa! Let's go see Papa!"

"Nice work," said Marti, as she wiped the maple syrup off of Lilly's face and helped her out of her chair.

"I thought so, too," laughed Carmen. "Bye-bye Lilly!" Carmen was very proud of her little matchmaker moments. They didn't happen very often, but they always made her feel a little adventuresome. The room was noisy and filled with excitement. This was going to be a good day, she thought. Lisa seemed very fond of Carmen, which delighted both of them, and also Lisa's grateful parents.

Caroline hurriedly entered the dining room and went straight for another cup of coffee. Checking in with Carmen, she found it sweet to see her with a baby. She made her way over to Julia and David, gave them both a hug and then moved on to find Brad and Jarrod. They were sharing a table with Michelle and Lauren Greene.

"Mom!" called out Jarrod. "Over here!" Both of her sons rose from the table as she arrived. "Will you join us? Let me get you a chair." Jarrod moved his place setting over and gave his mother his seat, he then brought over another chair, placing it near her. Lauren and Michelle seemed to be enjoying their breakfast with Brad and Jarrod, as the four of them had been recalling their days in North Carolina together. Caroline smiled at each "*Remember when*"...story.

"Where are your parents?" asked Caroline

"They wanted to sleep in this morning, which is almost unheard of for my father. By now, he's usually already been to the gym and is ready for breakfast," answered Michelle.

"Let them sleep as long as they want," said Caroline. "There's plenty for all of you to do here without them." Caroline caught Carmen's eye and nodded a signal for her to speak. She handed off baby Lisa to her mother and stood in the center of the room, drawing everyone's attention.

"Caroline and I want you to enjoy the beauty of AngelFire as we finish our preparations for the wedding. We have made arrangements that offer you a few options. You have your choice of golf at the country club, a tram-ride to the top of the mountain, horseback riding, or hiking to the lake for a picnic. Lunches will be provided at all four destinations. For those who are brave and adventuresome, we have arranged for hot air balloon rides for tomorrow morning! Please sign up at the front desk, where a person from our staff will give you the details. Enjoy your day – but please remember to return in time to join us at the wedding service at 7:00 pm."

The chatter began immediately as choices were discussed and decisions were made. Brad leaned toward his mother and asked

"Before you go off somewhere again, can I speak with you for a few minutes?"

"Of course, actually if you'll walk with me, I'd like to make a quick trip outside to check on a few things," answered Caroline. She kissed Michelle and Lauren and thanked them for coming for this wedding weekend, promising them more merriment ahead. Jarrod elected to stay behind with the girls, then Brad and his mother walked out arm in arm. From across the room, Ric watched them, proudly.

"So what is it? Is your dad snoring? Do you want me to find him another room?" asked Caroline.

"No – dad doesn't snore..." said Brad. "Mom, Jarrod and I have been thinking, and last night we spoke to Erik about it. We want your permission to evaluate Aunt Nicole's math and science media project and consider finishing it, and want Erik to look at the graphics. I think that with a collaboration of the three of us, we may be able to save it and possibly make something of real value out of it."

Caroline stopped abruptly and squared off with her eldest son.. "You could, you would, do that?"

"Yes, I really think we can," he answered.

"Does your father know about this?"

"No, there wasn't any reason to talk to him until we got your permission to take a look at everything. We know that you have all the data and recordings."

Caroline put her arms around Brad's neck and said, "After this weekend is over, I'll give you and Jarrod everything. It is all upstairs in a safe place. Nicole would have loved this, absolutely loved this!" She hugged her son tightly and said, "Just have a good time this weekend and when you leave, you can take it all with you. I know this will make your dad and Lila happy, too."

Chapel in the Woods

"I dreamed of a wedding of elaborate elegance,
A chapel filled with family and friends.
I asked him what kind of a wedding he wished for,
He said one that would make me his wife."

~Author Unknown

C aroline continued her walk toward the western edge of the grand lawns, which was bordered by a stand of golden aspens. A crew of eight men were busily assembling a pavilion that would soon become a sanctuary framed in the glory of nature. The golden aspens provided a natural border to the right and a trio of forty-five foot tall pines were flanked on the left. The chapel framework had been constructed and was crowned in a white covering, while the sides were clear enough to incorporate the encircling beauty of the setting.

Electricians were installing the centerpiece chandelier, along with carefully disguised perimeter and platform lighting. More of the crew had begun setting down the walnut parquet flooring.

A pathway was being smoothed and prepared for lanterns and flowers. The industrious crew barely acknowledged her presence.

Thoroughly pleased with their progress, Caroline was anxious for the floral teams to arrive as they had much to accomplish in an afternoon. Just as she reached for her cell phone to call them, she caught a glimpse of the incoming trucks. A few minutes later, the crews were introduced to each other and began to coordinate their design plans. She decided that it might be a good time to check on the progress over at the APAC room where staff members were preparing for the reception. Some of the florist's team followed her over to survey the room. To her delight, the newly finished dance floor was protected with brown paper while they set up tables and chairs around the perimeter. A local electrician was hanging hundreds of miniature lights which would create a starlit room. The florist's teams decided to split up with half working on the chapel and half working on the reception room. As their work got underway, Caroline walked back to the Inn to see if all the guests were enjoying the activities offered for the day. Carmen met her in the foyer and they walked to her office together. "Is everyone gone?"

"Almost," said Carmen. "Julia, David, Ric and Brad are a foursome at the golf course; Erik, Laney and their little girls went on a picnic with Kate and Sigrid; Diana, Jackson, Michelle and Lauren are on their way up the mountain, along with Marti and 'Papa' Erik."

"What about Jarrod?" asked Caroline.

"Well, Jarrod was with me when we received a call from Sigrid's daughter Sherri about an hour ago. She'll be here at noon!"

"Jarrod wanted to be here when Sherri and her daughters arrived. I'm not sure why, but he thinks this will be a reunion he shouldn't miss."

Jarrod had had a crush on Sherri from the time he was in preschool," said Caroline. "Wait – where are we going to put her?"

"I will work it out," said Carmen. "Remember, the Amoroso brothers are going to stay at Robbie's ski condo, which gave us two extra rooms, just in case."

"Things are going to get crazy-busy here at noon, but don't worry, it always seems to work."

"What do you mean?" said Caroline.

"At noon, we are expecting Paula and the band, along with the cellist Camille; at noon we are now expecting Sherri and her two daughters who will see the amazing transformation of the new Ms. Sigrid; at noon, Siggy is expecting the wedding cake and its creator Arturo, which will no doubt spark another conversation and at noon we are expecting the groom and my missing husband to show up with the unpredictable Amoroso brothers."

"At noon?" she asked.

"At noon!" she answered.

And after a brief moment...Caroline said, "Why don't you come with me to take a look at the chapel."

"I'd love to. Do you think that when we get there we should get on our knees and pray?"

"All the way there and all the way back, too," said Caroline.

When the two women approached the chapel, they were taken aback by the progress that had been accomplished.

"This will take the bride's breath away," said Carmen. "It is going to be so elegant."

"I'm considering having the photographer take some pictures before the wedding, just in case we ever decide to do this again, or want to create other weddings in the future," said Caroline.

"Now you are sounding like Frank," noted Carmen.

The floor was finished and polished. The aubergine colored carpet for the aisle had been rolled out. Dozens of eight foot curly willow branches were affixed to each of the supporting posts. Small crystal votive candles were being hung from the thicker branches. Bolts of linen in aubergine and ivory were transforming the dais. The fabric was draped and swagged, transforming the area where the ceremony would transpire. The risers were covered in the same carpet and a clear Lucite lectern was centered upon them. Tall standing candelabras were placed on either side of the platform and were awaiting their floral décor. The chairs were placed, but their linen coverings were still on hangers and in plastic bags.

The flowers had not been brought out of the truck yet, but Caroline was able to visualize it all. Deep red and purple leaves from Japanese maples would be combined with honey-colored roses, green cymbidiums, rusty dahlias, ginger stems and pheasant feathers.

It appeared to Caroline that at least the setting would be exactly as she had hoped for, though other things were surely turning out differently. She had promised Kate a beautiful wedding and this chapel would provide a graceful autumn sunset ceremony.

Carmen looked at her watch and said, "It's time for me to get back to my station. I don't want to miss a thing and I want to fix myself up a little before my husband gets here."

"I'd like to find my son before he sees Sherri," said Caroline.

As they walked toward the Inn, they received simultaneous text messages from JB & Robbie. *"Sorry- running late, problem with tailor, the four of us should arrive by three - Sorry"*

Carmen's face turned red. Caroline's face turned white.

High Noon

"And the tide was against us, it was noon when we arrived there."

- Christopher Columbus

*C*aroline found Jarrod in the great room. He had on a fresh shirt and he looked like he had just shaved. He was wearing his dad's cologne. Her sweet boy, who seemed to have difficulty finding a nice girlfriend, was about to reunite with a longtime object of a boyhood crush. Sherri Kerrington was older, taller, hipper and cooler than Jarrod, in his eyes. In Caroline's eyes, Sherri was an original California *"Valley Girl"*.

"Hello handsome," she said as she greeted her son with a kiss. "So you stayed behind? Didn't any of our excursion options appeal to you today?"

"I signed up for one of the hot air balloon rides for tomorrow," answered Jarrod. "Mom, you heard that Sherri will be here soon, right?"

"I did, and she's bringing her daughters with her."

"Is she bringing her husband Michael?"

"Apparently not, according to Carmen."

"Well, it will be good to see her. It's been at least a year. They go to their house in Durango a lot, so she hasn't been in LA as much," said Jarrod.

"Jarrod, things have not been going very smoothly between Sherri and her mother recently. Hopefully, she will want to have some private time with her in order to work out some of their differences. Sigrid is a different person since she now owns a thriving business."

"She's a different person in a number of ways, mom. I think Sherri's in for a shock!"

"More than one, Jarrod," said Caroline. They both caught the view of a familiar red SUV coming up the drive toward the entrance. "There they are now." She and Jarrod went out to greet them.

"Jarrod!" said Sherri, as she threw her arms around his shoulders. "It's been too long. You look great!" Her warm greeting evoked a grand smile from Jarrod. He went to the other side of the car and helped her two little girls in yellow daisy printed dresses out of the car.

Caroline welcomed Sherri, and then directed her attention toward the girls. "You both look so pretty in your lovely dresses!"

"I wanted to wear my red boots," pouted little Jenney.

"When I was six years old, all I wanted was to wear my boots, too," said Caroline. Jenney became her instant friend. "What about you Mattie? Would you rather wear your boots, today?"

"I picked out these dresses and they are perfectly fine," said Mattie, much the eight year old fashion diva.

"Okay then, shall we find our room?" said Caroline. She took them through the entrance and up to the front desk where Carmen was waiting with a key to their room – *the last room in at the Inn!*

"Where's my mother?" asked Sherri.

"She's at a picnic on the lake with Erik and Laney and their girls. Kate is there, too. I don't think she knew that you were coming," said Caroline.

"Oh...okay. Can't we stay with her in one of the bungalows or is she sharing with one of her friends?"

"Sharing," said Caroline.

"Oh...okay, then where are we staying?"

"Looks like your room is right next to mine!" said Jarrod with that same smile again.

Great – thought Caroline.

"Oh good!" said Sherri. "Come on girls. Let's get settled in and then we'll find grandma."

"I'll help you," said Jarrod.

Great – thought Caroline, again.

Shortly after they ascended the staircase, Carmen received a call from the "Lulu Parr" Bungalow. "Sigrid? I thought you were at a picnic at the lake. I'm glad you called. I have a little news for you."

"I walked back early to get ready for Artie. He should be here in less than a half hour. I want to help him bring in the cake and set it up. What news do you have for me?"

"Sherri and your granddaughters are here. Caroline and Jarrod just took them upstairs to get settled in."

"I wasn't – I didn't know – I, uh...Carmen will you do a favor for me and direct them to the lake? I want to see Artie first – before I see my daughter. I'm not sure what to expect from her."

"Okay – this call never happened. I will send them off for a picnic on the lake. I'm sure Jarrod would love to take them the long way, too."

"Thank you, thank you, thank you!"

When Caroline, Jarrod, Sherri and the girls descended the stairs; they were greeted by Carmen, who was now holding a picnic basket. She handed it to Jarrod and asked him to take them on the scenic route to the lake. Caroline and Carmen locked eyes for an instant which was long enough to get the message. Little Jenny had her boots on – calling them her picnic boots. Her sibling told her that she looked ridiculous. Their mother was oblivious. Jarrod took the basket and walked with Sherri and her girls toward the lake.

"My hero," said Caroline as they exited.

"I think right now he's Siggy's hero," said Carmen. "Artie and the cake will be here in minutes! Let's ask them to put it in Lulu Parr's refrigerator. They can assemble it in their kitchen and get it over to the reception when we need it."

"Brilliant," said Caroline and as the word came out of her mouth she saw the S-S-Sweets van coming up the drive. "Give Siggy a quick ring! Let's get out there!"

Caroline and Carmen went out to the driveway with smiles so big, they should have given the driver a clue that they were up to something. They waved and pointed in the direction of Sigrid's bungalow.

"I think we need to be with her; she must be as nervous as a hen," said Caroline. And in that very moment, Caroline's cell phone rang. It was Paula, calling from the Lodge. They had just arrived, checked in and wanted a little rest from the trip. She thought she would bring the band over at 1:30 pm. Caroline suggested that they have lunch at the Summit Haus and look for Diana and Marti, then come over for a rehearsal at around 2:30 pm. Paula agreed that this suggestion would work out better for them as well.

"Okay, so everyone is here but the groom and my husband," said Carmen.

"Not to mention the brothers Amoroso," said Caroline, softly so only Carmen could hear her. "Let's just deal with what's in front of us. And.....heeeeerrrrreeesss Artie!"

"Artie! It's so good to see you! Welcome to AngelFire! I am so glad you could find us up here in the middle of God's country. I'd like to introduce you to Carmen Robles."

"Carmen, please meet Arturo Montecito."

"*Así que encantado de conocerte,*" said Carmen

"*El placer es todo mío,*" returned Arturo. He turned to Caroline and asked, "Where would you like the cake?"

"Let's take it inside the bungalow. It has a kitchen I think you can work with...we'll help you," said Caroline. She glanced at Carmen who suddenly could not take her eyes off Arturo. She cleared her throat, caught Carmen's attention and tilted her head twice toward the front door. Carmen took the smallest of the four cake boxes, while Arturo took the largest.

"Please be very careful with that one. It is the most especial of all of them," said Arturo.

"I promise to be very careful," she said, as she approached the entrance to the bungalow. She knocked twice and said, "Sigrid, we are coming in with the cake. Is that okay?"

"Yes, of course, please come in."

Carmen was a little confused as to why Sigrid didn't come out to the car to help. She placed the box on a kitchen counter. Then Sigrid entered the living room – and she saw her. She was dressed in a hot pink suit with cropped pants and Chanel jacket, with a red tank top and red sandals. "You look sensational!" She wanted to say more but it was too late.

He just stood there...staring at her. Carmen rushed over to take the box that looked like it was about to fall out of his hands.

"Well?" said Caroline.

"I am speechless...how could my beautiful Sigrid become even more beautiful? Wow! How? What have you..." He couldn't finish his sentence – he rushed toward her, then stopped short, took a look at her from head to toe and then embraced her – tenderly. Sigrid Kerrington cried.

"I think we should go now," whispered Caroline to Carmen, and they slipped out the front door.

"El es un hombre bien parecido! Muy guapo y tan joven!" Carmen mumbled to herself.

"I heard that and I understood it too. Siggy deserves another chance at love. Why shouldn't she be with someone younger?"

"I don't know how she focuses on her business with him around," said Carmen.

"Oh, I think she has her eyes wide open," said Caroline.

"It's nice to know that passion never dies," said Carmen.

"That's a lovely way to look at it. No one knows how this will end up for them.. You're right – it's nice to know there can be more to life, at any age," said Caroline.

"You, my friend, might have to get off this mountain for that!"

They grinned like schoolgirls all the way back to the Inn and came back to reality in about ten short minutes, when Caroline's cell phone rang. It was Jarrod, "Sherri's mom must be back at her bungalow, 'cause she's not here. Aunt Kate said she went to see about the wedding cake. The girls are having a great time with Erik's daughters. It's actually kinda cute, mom. Sherri seems awfully eager to see her mom. Is it okay to bring her back now?"

"Um...can you stall her for another ten or fifteen minutes and then walk back here? I'll call Sigrid and let her know you're coming. Just meet us in the great room."

"Okay, we'll meet you there in about forty-five minutes."

"Perfect," said Caroline. She made the call and left a message at Lulu Parr's.

Jarrod was diligent about watching the time and delayed their return from the lake as his mother requested. Erik and Laney offered to keep Jenny and Mattie with them, but Jenny wanted to see her grandma. She also wanted another ride on Jarrod's shoulders and he gladly obliged.

"I'm glad you chose to come to the wedding," he said to Sherri.

"We were in Durango, and it was kind of a last minute decision. I packed last night and we took off at about eight this morning and drove straight through. It's not that far. The girls have their video games and we have DVD players in the headrests for the back seat. They are pretty good little travelers."

"Why didn't Michael come with you?" asked Jarrod.

"He's in LA...can I tell you something in confidence?

"Of course."

"Well,....Jarrod, we're kind of separated right now," said Sherri.

"I'm sorry to hear that, Sherri. When did this happen?"

"About seven months ago. Nothing's official – yet anyway." She pointed her finger upwards to indicate that the little one on his shoulders might be listening.

"Do you want to get down and walk, Jenny?" she asked.

"Okay, but only if you let me lead the way," said Jenny proudly, and she stomped ahead in her red cowgirl boots.

"Jarrod, I came because I have to make amends with my mother. According to my husband, I have treated her and just about everyone else we know quite badly. He's said he's sick of my self-centeredness, and he's elected me as the poster girl for Narcissists Anonymous. I've been in therapy ever since he left.......Please don't tell anyone about this."

"This doesn't sound like Michael, at all. Does he see the girls?"

"Yes, he sees them twice a week on Sundays and Wednesdays. He doesn't keep them for the night, which makes me think he has someone else in his life. If everything he's said is true, I wouldn't blame him if he does have someone else. I don't know how all this is going to turn out, but I do know that I need to fix things with my mother. He was right about that. My therapist has a 'to-do' list for me, and this is definitely in the top three."

"Are you all right? Is Michael supporting the three of you?"

"As long as I am in therapy and working on myself, he supports us completely, but I do know that well may run dry one day, and I will have to get a job. Both of the girls are in school now, so I can try to get something during the day. This has been hard... really hard, and hopefully, if I can at least work things out with my mother, I can reward myself by having a good time tonight – for the first time in months!"

Caroline and Sigrid were in the great room having a glass of wine and waiting for Sherri and Jarrod. Caroline had used the forty-five minutes to check on the progress of the chapel and reception details. Fortunately, Arturo wanted to freshen up after his long and tedious drive.

"This will be interesting, seeing Sherri after months and months of no communication. I wonder what made her decide to come up here after all," said Sigrid.

"Maybe she just wanted to break the ice within the safety of all the rest of us around her."

"I have missed my granddaughters, but I've been so focused on the business and Artie, that well, I haven't really missed Sherri much. Is that too terrible to say?"

"It's real, and let's not underestimate how much you have accomplished this year."

"She has always been difficult. Some children just come into this world with attitudes that make you wonder what planet they came from. I used to have a few of them in my daycare business, too. It helps to know you're not the only one, while you've been thinking that it must be your fault. I know Sherri too well to think she is here because she misses me. When that girl was a baby and started rolling in her crib – she rolled *away* from me. When she learned to walk – she walked *away* from me. 'Come to mama' was never a phrase she responded to very well." Sigrid and Caroline's conversation stopped and their heads turned when they heard the doors open in the foyer. They heard Jenney's voice first.

"Gramma – where are youuuuu?"

"I'm in heeeeere," answered Sigrid.

Little Jenney ran toward the voice but stopped cold in her tracks as they entered the great room.

Jarrod and Sherry were a few steps behind her. As Sherry entered the room she said to Caroline, "Have you seen my – MOTHER ??? Oh my God!! – I – I – I – What have you done to yourself?? Oh my...."

Jarrod immediately stepped in and said "Doesn't she look beautiful?"

Sherri started to cry and Sigrid froze. Then Jenny said, "You *not* my gramma."

Caroline stepped forward and said, "Yes, she is your same grandma in her heart. She's just looks a lot slimmer and younger now, sweetheart. She's just even more beautiful!"

Sigrid walked toward her daughter and put her arms around her, "Why are you crying?"

"I'm sorry mother, I am so sorry. Look at you...you look amazing and you've obviously done all this all by yourself. Michael was right...I haven't been there for you in any way this year. Jarrod tells me your business is very successful and that you are taking good care of yourself. I have been such a terrible daughter. I'm sorry for everything, really I am." Sherri's makeup was streaking down her cheeks, which reminded Caroline of a scene between Sigrid and Sherri in reverse, just one year ago."

Jarrod went over to the wine set up and poured a glass of cabernet for himself and a pinot gris for Sherri. She gratefully accepted it. He invited all of them to sit down again, but before they were seated, they heard the entry doors and all heads turned to see who was about to join them. Arturo Montecito glided into the room and went straight to Sigrid's side. "You must be Sherri. Allow me to introduce myself; I am Arturo." He kissed Sherri's hand and continued, "I have heard much about you, and you are almost as beautiful as your mother." He placed his arm around Sigrid gave her a little squeeze, which evoked a little giggle."

Caroline stood motionless. Fortunately Jarrod caught Sherri *mid-faint* before her head hit the floor.

Separate and Together

"Today is the tomorrow you worried about yesterday"

Anonymous

*J*ust outside the front entrance of the Inn, Erik, Laney and the children, along with Kate, met Sigrid and Arturo, who had Sherri's daughter Jenny, with them. Jarrod had taken Sherri up to her room to recover. Apparently, all the new developments in her mother's life were too much for her.

After introductions were made, Kate said, "Siggy, you've been holding out on me. I don't believe you told me how charming Arturo is. I don't think Robbie has ever kissed my hand." She turned to Arturo, and added, "It's been a pleasure to meet you and I look forward to getting to know you." It took some coaxing for Mattie to join her sister, but she acquiesced and joined Jenny for a trip to grandma's bungalow to see Lulu Parr. Erik and Laney took their daughters upstairs for a nap before the wedding.

Kate joined Carmen and Caroline in the great room. They both were holding clipboards with checklists. "Wow!" she said as she entered the room. "Now there's a hunka-burning-love."

"You must have met Arturo," said Carmen. "He's very attractive. I'm happy for Siggy. Have you heard from the groom?"

"No – Should I have?"

"I guess I'm just not used to not knowing where my husband is every minute of the day," said Carmen. "And I also guess that comes with our working together all these years."

"Stop worrying," said Caroline, "And let's not let the bride be concerned on her wedding day! Katie, I'd like to have you get ready for the wedding upstairs in my apartment. So if you'll go get your dress and everything else, and meet me upstairs at about three o'clock, we can get started. Marti and Diana will have returned from their trip up the mountain by then. Carmen, you are welcome to join us. There's room for all of us."

"Talking JB Robles into wearing the new suit I bought for him may take a while. We'll join you at the chapel at six to help with any last minute details," said Carmen.

"I tremble to think how I would ever do anything like this without you two. Seriously, my knees get wobbly," said Caroline.

"She's joking Katie. Trust me, Caroline has become a master planner. I can't wait for you to see what she has prepared for you."

"*Uh – huh-huh, no details,*" said Caroline. In the periphery of her vision, she caught sight of an AngelFire guest van approaching. She drew closer to the window to see which group was returning from their excursion. When she saw her son Brad exiting the van, she excused herself and went out to greet them.

"Mom, for the first time, I beat dad at golf!" he said as he greeted her and wrapped an arm around her for half a hug.

"He's become quite a good player," said Julia. "David and I both are impressed, aren't we David?" David nodded and smiled, then went on grumbling something about not having his own clubs.

Ric came around from the other side of the van and commented on the strength of youth, and added another *"attaboy"* to the conversation. The group seemed to have thoroughly enjoyed their day together. Julia and David were ready for a rest from the day and agreed to meet at the chapel at six-forty-five. Ric offered to assist Caroline with any last minute details, which was something for a *"we have people for that"* kind of guy. Caroline appreciated and duly noted that he had made genuine efforts to show her a newer side of himself. He also agreed to meet with her and the Robles at six o'clock.

Brad had shared his ideas regarding Nicole's project with his dad. Ric deeply appreciated that all three of the boys were willing to try and save Nicole's work and he was not surprised that Caroline had agreed. He hoped to have one of his UCLA alumni friends monitor their progress. This had the potential to become an excellent family project and possibly bring all of them together more frequently.

About the time they were each headed back to their rooms, a small bus loaded with musicians and instruments made its way up the drive. The temperature was about sixty-eight degrees, and yet the driver found it necessary to wear a pair of old-fashioned earmuffs, apparently to muffle the noise. The teens dashed out of the bus as soon as it stopped and Paula had them lined up beside it in a flash. A woman with very long, very curly, red hair with tiny flowers in it, wearing a long black velvet dress, stepped outside the bus and joined Paula. Camille looked as Irish as the bride with features that said she could have been Kate's cousin.

Carmen joined Caroline to welcome them. They were first introduced to Camille MacArthur, a cellist, who would play for the ceremony and dinner. The teen musicians were already dressed in their performance attire in black pants and skirts and crisp white shirts and blouses. They were so excited they could hardly maintain the disciplined manners they normally exhibited. A pizza party and night away in a hotel; performing with their conductor at a private party; a trip to part of New Mexico they had never seen before; – and on top of it all they were going to be paid! Caroline and Carmen led the way to the chapel, where Camille set up her cello. Several of them bowed at the end of an aisle, crossed themselves and were nearly silent as they patiently took their seats. Carmen sat with the teens, whispering Spanish to those who preferred it and English to the others. Paula returned to her charges and informed them that they would be able to attend the service and partake of the wedding dinner as guests. Afterward, they would perform the dance music as planned.

The troop was led to the AngelFire Performing Arts Center for an on sight rehearsal. All instruments were set up on the stage behind curtains. Two students, who normally played the violin in the youth orchestra, would play alongside Camille for the dinner music.

Paula left the teens backstage to warm up and circled back to find Caroline. She found her with Chef Niccolini, who was completing the training for what appeared to be a rather large number of wait staff. Carmen was attending the training as she would be their *"go- to"* person when necessary.

Paula asked Caroline for a moment, alone. "This room is absolutely enchanting, Caroline. It's barely recognizable! My kids are thrilled. Thank you for all you are doing for them. These are great musicians, and I know they won't disappoint you."

"I'm certain they'll be wonderful. I've asked the photographer to take extra photos of them and he will send an extra set of copies directly to you. I hope they won't mind if others join them during the evening. I had the piano tuned, too and was hoping we could coax Marti to play a little something with them."

"They would be honored!" said Paula.

"Camille is quite the elegant woman. Is she from Albuquerque?" asked Caroline.

"She's from Boston, and she just finished playing the opera season in Santa Fe," answered Paula. "Camille also works with high schools through the GSA Network, on an anti-bullying campaign."

"Another activist! I love it!" said Caroline. "That's impressive... it sounds like we're lucky to have her with us tonight," said

Caroline. "Paula, I hope you'll stay an extra few days up here before your winter concert season begins. I know that you work very hard, and your music takes up most of your time; but you've been invited to be part of a wonderful family of friends, and we all want to see you happy again. Please don't separate yourself from us in your grief."

"I will come up again, soon. I promise," said Paula. Nothing more needed to be said.

Caroline walked back toward the Inn and watched as the second guest van returned the Greene family and Marti with Erik, from their expedition up the mountain. The sounds of their laughter confirmed that they had enjoyed their afternoon. Diana waved when she saw Caroline.

"I trust you all had a beautiful trip?" asked Caroline. They all responded at once regarding the breathtaking vistas on their way up the mountain and the tranquil hike down. She also sensed that Marti and Erik seemed a little – or maybe even a lot more comfortable together. Jackson headed for the bungalow for a little relaxation, which meant a nap. The Greene girls headed for their rooms pledging long hot baths. Diana confirmed their time to meet with the bride in Caroline's apartment. Marti decided she would also join them and went to the "May Lillie" bungalow to get the bride and all her things.

Within minutes Kate and Marti were at the entrance. Kate held her dress high over her head, not to let it touch the ground. Marti came up behind her with a large suitcase filled with *God-knows-what* a bride think she needs. Caroline rounded up two staff members to take the suitcase and belongings up to her apartment. Kate accepted Caroline's invitation to indulge herself in her steeping tub, and brought an herbal potion of her own making for a deep immersion in luxury. Marti supervised the transport then left Katie to bathe and returned to the great room where Diana and Caroline were having tea.

It was at about 3:15pm when Carmen joined them clipboard in hand and confirmed that everything seemed in order for the reception. "I heard the band rehearse a little, they're terrific! I may even get my husband to dance with me tonight!" She was the first one to see the limousine. "Speaking of my husband... this must be them, now."

"Well I'm glad the bride is upstairs," said Marti. The four women rose and went outside to greet the missing groom and his party.

The limousine stopped in front of the "May Lillie" bungalow and parked. The uniformed driver opened the side door to let his passengers get out. The first to step out was Giovanni, the Best Man. His charcoal tuxedo was obviously custom made. He looked as if he just stepped out of an Armani ad. In true Amoroso tradition, he adjusted his deep plum silk tie and his sunglasses, but then of course, he did not remove them.

The four women waiting at the entrance found the view splendid.

The second tall, dark and handsome to exit the limo was Antonio, who was a little taller and more muscular than his brother Giovanni. He too would make his tailor and his hair stylist proud. He wore the same color silk tie, but made in a damask weave.

"Maravilloso...maybe that's why Frank didn't bring them here," said Carmen under her breath.

"Yes, indeed," said Diana.

"Rev?" said Marti.

"In the image and likeness of....," said Diana.

The third to exit the limo was the groom, a little shorter than his two brothers but yet again, in a no-doubt custom made tuxedo in a gun metal grey. The groom's tie was a deeper shade, closer to aubergine. Robbie Collicci beamed.

"These Amoroso boys must have left a thousand dollars with their hairstylist, last night," said Marti. The other women just stood their smiling...big, wide smiles.

The fourth man to exit the limo was significantly taller, with broader shoulders with more of a tan, impeccably tailored, in a slightly lighter shade of grey. Undoubtedly he used the same hairstylist, though his style was slightly longer than the groom's. He repeated the same gestures of adjusting his grey silk tie, blending with his grey shirt, suit and shoes. And of course he too did not remove his sunglasses.

"I thought Sal wasn't com...," started Caroline...as she and Carmen simultaneously dropped their clipboards.

While the first three men went into "May Lillie's" bungalow, the fourth man walked directly toward the four women. Marti wisely covered her mouth; Diana's was in a full, broad smile, while Carmen's was gaping.

JB Robles extended his hand to his wife and said, "Hello beautiful. May I escort you to the O'Neil - Collicci wedding this evening?" He swooped his wife off of her feet and walked in the direction of their place. "We'll meet you at the chapel at six," he shouted back over his shoulder.

"¡Dios mío," was all they heard.

Let - all of us - eat cake!

"The most dangerous food is wedding cake."

James Thurber

"What is it with all the men up here this weekend?" said Marti.

"I have no idea, but I'm certainly enjoying the additional scenery on my trip to AngelFire this year," said Diana. "I think this will be one fine-looking wedding party."

"Speaking of fine-looking men, I think that while Katie is soaking in Love Potion #9, I will check on Arturo and the wedding cake before we begin helping her get ready," said Caroline.

"You mean there is another one? Mercy!" said Diana.

As Caroline started to leave the room, Sigrid came through the entrance with her two granddaughters.

"It's time to find my mommy," said Jenny to Caroline.

"We've got to get ready for the wedding silly," said Mattie.

"I'll take them upstairs," said Marti. "Then I'll go up to your place and make sure the bride has not fallen asleep in that tub."

"Why don't you come with us and see the cake," said Sigrid to Diana. "Then you can meet Artie."

"Brace yourself Rev," said Marti with a wink.

Caroline and Diana followed Sigrid into her bungalow which had open pastry boxes all over the kitchen counters. In the center of the table was a four-tiered work of art – the wedding cake. The ivory fondant had been overlaid with an additional design replicating the vintage lace on Kate's wedding gown and the cake was accented with minute pearl borders. Roses, tiny orchids, lilies, and miniature parrot tulips with wisps of ivy gracefully cascaded from the top to the base.

"I wanted to set the top on the cake after we take it over there," said Arturo as he entered the room.

"It's stunning," said Caroline. "She will love this."

"Diana, I don't think you have met Artie yet," said Sigrid

"Amazing... Artie, this cake is absolutely exquisite," said Diana. "You are quite the artist."

"Thank you. I haven't made one of these in a long time, and certainly never before without consulting with the bride. This is a very unusual," said Arturo.

"Indeed, as much of the weekend has been so far," said Caroline. "This beauty has a vintage look and is exactly like the kind of cake Katie would have chosen. I think she'll be extremely pleased. What have you designed for the top of the cake?"

Arturo left the room for a moment and returned with another pastry box. From it, he removed a pair of delicate swans facing each other, heads bowed tenderly toward one another.

"They're divine," said Diana.

Caroline looked at Arturo tearfully and said, "Flawless."

"They're made of white chocolate and hand painted," said Sigrid. "So are all those flowers."

"I didn't realize that," said Diana, as she took a second look at them. "The details are incredible. I don't think I can bear to see them eaten tonight."

"Siggy, how did you two find each other?" asked Diana.

"Kismet," said Arturo.

"And Craigslist," added Sigrid.

"Let's transport this to the reception room before it gets any later. You can set the swans and we can all get ready for the wedding," said Caroline. She called Chef Niccolini who sent over two staff members with a cart. Along with Arturo, the three of them placed his sculptured confectionary in a safe place.

Diana and Caroline agreed to meet at her apartment at four o'clock to prepare the bride. Sigrid and Arturo would meet them at the chapel at six-forty-five.

Robles Revelations

"Money isn't the most important thing in life, but it's reasonably close to oxygen on the "gotta have it" scale."

<u>*Zig Ziglar*</u>

*A*bout forty feet into the journey toward their home, Carmen said, "Okay, you can put me down now...I can walk the rest of the way."

"Thank you," said JB, nearly breathless. They said nothing until they reached threshold of their home. "May I?" he asked. She nodded and he carried her into their living room and placed her gently on the sofa. "There – that's because I never did it when I should have." He waited for a response from Carmen, but got nothing. So he decided he better start talking...fast.

"I want to tell you everything...where I've been...what we did... all of it, but first you have to promise me that you will not say a word until I am finished. Can you do that for me?"

"This better be good," said Carmen.

"Carmen...you're already talking."

"Okay – okay – talk."

"First, I want to tell you that I just had the time of my life. Those are the craziest guys I've ever met and I've never laughed so hard in my life! And I saw another side of life I have never seen before – ever. And I learned something... something important.

Yesterday, when I got to Robbie's house in Santa Fe, those guys were eating lunch and just waiting for me. There was an argument going on and Robbie said he didn't want a party and was not going to go to Las Vegas with them. They promised him there was no party planned and that we were all just going to their brother Sal's house. This argument wasn't nasty or anything, but those guys are relentless and they just don't take 'no' for an answer. As soon as we finished eating, we all got in a limousine and were taken to the airport, where they had a private plane waiting. It was waiting there for them just to finish the argument, all that time! I've never been on a private plane before. Frank and I used to fly in commercial planes, just like everyone else. There was leather everywhere and plush carpets, and we even had a waitress serving us drinks and food. *Don't give me that look – I didn't have any drinks.*

About an hour later, we were getting into another limo and were headed for Sal's house. I have no idea where we were, just somewhere high up with an incredible hundred and eighty degree view. His place was huge with a lot of glass and stone, everywhere. Nothing like AngelFire; It was real modern.

Then Sal came out to greet us and I almost dropped to my knees, because he looks so much like Frank. I've met him once before, but I guess I just forgot how much those two looked alike. It took me a few minutes, you know what I mean? *Don't answer me.*

After Sal and Robbie talked for a few minutes about business, uh – in another room, they came out and Sal said he had a wedding gift for Robbie and a little something for everybody else, too. We followed him down a hallway where he opened a door and there were two men with measuring tapes around their necks and four women sitting at sewing machines. They were going to make suits for us – overnight! Can you imagine that? I said *"no"* at first but like I said, these guys don't take *'no'* for an answer. So we were all in our skivvies with these two men, who were measuring us, choosing fabrics, shirts and suggesting shoes. They even made our ties! Those people were there to make us suits – overnight! Have you ever heard of that? *Don't answer me.*

Then Giovanni, who's a really great guy said he had a gift for Robbie and all the rest of us at his place, but they wanted to go out to dinner first. So Sal got his driver to take us to the restaurant, which again, I have no idea where it was or the even name of the place. It was very dark, and one of those places where celebrities can go without being bothered. They gave us menus with no prices on them. I guess it was one of those places where if you had to ask...you shouldn't be there. They ordered food like it was their last supper! These guys can eat! So I ate right along with them. I even ate a few things I never heard of before, too. *Don't look at me like that.*

Next, Antonio talked Giovanni into calling *"the girls"* and asking them to come back in the morning. He thought we should go to some shows. *Don't look at me like that – it's not what you think.*

We finished eating and we went to a comedy magic thing, which was funny and really amazing. Then we went to see Viva Elvis, or something like that. Elvis is still *The King* in Las Vegas. It was great. Then we went to see this woman named Rita something. She was hilarious; she said things like, *'I love being married. It's so great to find that one special person you want to annoy for the rest of your life.'* She was funny, but the Amoroso brothers were just as funny.

They told funny stories about Robbie and some both funny and interesting stuff about Frank. I guess Frank never liked to spend money. They never knew why. Unlike his brothers Frank was quiet and was not the party animal these guys are. They said that when Frank left the family business they worried about him so much that each one of them privately sent Frank money each month. Eventually, they figured out that they were all sending him money and he was just putting it in the bank! They thought it was hilarious! Sal said, *'I bet Frankie still had his first communion money in the bank'.* Pretty interesting – huh? – *No need to answer that.*

So now it has to be after one o'clock in the morning, and all I want to do is go to bed and these guys want to do a little gambling. *'Good for business',* they said. Gambling! You know I don't do any of that stuff, so I told them I was going to go sit in the bar. Then Giovanni hands me a handful of chips and I don't mean potato chips... and says to me *'Lighten up Chief, go make some money!'* So I had no idea how much I had or what to do with them. I walked over to a roulette table and put all my chips on one square! And I won!– just like that!

Robbie finally stands up and says *'Guys – I'm getting married tomorrow. I need to get some sleep tonight.'* Then Antonio says, *'We sure don't want you to fall asleep on your wedding night – So okay!'* So Robbie and I go back to Sal's and stay there, with a promise to be at Giovanni's for breakfast in the morning.

My mind was reeling with everything we had done, and how freely these guys spend money. They act like they have no worries or concerns about money, no lack of it and no limitations on spending it. The world is at their feet and they kept saying things like *'hey -it's just money'.* And I realize that they're not buying happiness with their money; they just *are* happy. Robbie says they're serious when they need to be serious and happy almost all the rest of the time. They think that life is supposed to be that way. It's hard to argue with that!

It made me look at how living in poverty as a kid set me up with some attitudes that have affected the rest of my life. And even though we don't have any money problems anymore, I still act like I'm that kid. I'm afraid it's temporary or that somehow we're going to lose it. Frank and I never talked much about money. He paid us well and fairly and I always felt like we earned it, so that worked for me. He and Robbie both have spoken about their *'crazy brothers',* but I'm not so sure they're so crazy. I think they just do what makes them happy. They live a high lifestyle, and that keeps them happy. They don't take life so seriously. I'm not sure they're so crazy after all.

Now I'm not saying that I could ever live their kind of life...but I sure understand now, why you do all the shopping you do and maybe why I was so resentful about it. But shop baby, shop! I don't want to change our lives or leave AngelFire or anything like that, but I do want to change a few things about me. So with that I finally went to sleep for a few hours. *Thank you for smiling at that....but I'm not done.*

At seven-thirty this morning, I dragged myself out of bed and took a shower and joined Robbie and Sal for coffee. The '*suit shop*' was still going. We went to Giovanni's. He lives in a penthouse suite, at a hotel, which again was huge, with another incredible view. The guys joined us and we all had a big breakfast together. Those guys must work out a lot to eat as much as they do and still look so good. They probably all have personal trainers.

So then.... '*the girls*' came in. Everybody seemed to know each other and - guess what? These women were hairstylists! That's when things got really uncomfortable for me. I said I'd sit out this part of the party and, as I said before, they don't take '*no*' for an answer. They told me it was time to join the twenty-first century, which you have said before, several times, I know. After all I had realized about myself in the night, I decided that if I really wanted to change myself...I could start right there and then, with a haircut. And they actually made a ceremony out of it. So we all got our hair cut and styled. Robbie was up for a change, too.

Then it was time to go back to Sal's and get into our new suits. When we got there, everything was laid out for us – Suits, shirts, ties and shoes. I don't even want to think about what all of this must have cost. The two tailors were our 'dressers' and we all got ready like a bunch of kids getting ready for a prom. But this was for Robbie's wedding and Robbie was giving his brothers instructions on how to behave. '*AngelFire is not Las Vegas*', he said several times.

So this is me, the new me. I know I look different, but I hope I can think different, too. We need to have more fun with our money, too.

And this is the truth about what happened to me in Las Vegas... Every place I went to...I wanted you to be there...I wanted you to see Sal's big house and Giovanni's penthouse. At the shows we saw, I thought you should be seeing them with me, and even the food we ate, I thought - you should been enjoying eating it, too. *I wanted you there with me.*

One more thing...when I won that money, I went back to Giovanni to give him back the chips and he wouldn't take them. I told him I didn't want to gamble anymore so he says to me *'Go do what every other red blooded man in America does when he wins like that. Go buy your wife something.'* So I cashed in my chips and I found out that I had won over $5,000. I found the shops and finally found a jewelry store. That's when I called you! – Remember? *No need to answer that.*

I have something for you. I don't know that it will fit right or even if you will like it, and you can take it back if you like. You've never had anything like this before, and I'm not used to buying anything like this..."

JB pulled a small pouch out of his pocket and placed a full carat, pear-shaped, diamond ring on Carmen's third finger, left hand. "You can talk now," he said.

"Before I kiss you," said Carmen, "Will you PLEASE take off those sunglasses?"

A Natural Woman

"Ain't it Good to Know You've Got a Friend"

- Carole King

*D*iana and Caroline climbed the stairs, declaring their pledge to make the bride look like a "million dollars". *God knows the groom does already*, thought Diana. As they entered Caroline's apartment, they found Kate in a bathrobe with a towel around her head and her feet up on an ottoman. The whole apartment was filled with a heady, sensual scent.

"What is that fragrance?" asked Caroline.

"It's an essential oil, and it's my own recipe," said Kate.

"Of course it is," said Marti, who was also sitting in an AngelFire robe with her feet up.

"And will you be sharing that recipe?" asked Diana.

"Not tonight, but if it works like it's supposed to, then I'll send you some for Christmas."

"Well I think it's intoxicating! If the groom likes it as much as I do, you'll be leaving the reception early!" said Diana. "Let's get your hair done first. I'll do your make up and then I'll have to leave, so I can get ready, too."

"Okay ladies, I want to look beautiful, but I still want to look like me," said Kate.

"You can do anything you want with my hair and makeup," said Marti. "I'm not sure who I am today or who I want to be tonight."

"I noticed something very tender passing between you and Erik on the mountain, today" said Diana. "He seemed to hang on your every word at lunch, too."

"I definitely felt my heart open a little today, which honestly, was a little uncomfortable for me. I've let my son and his wife and babies in, and that's pretty much it."

"Marti, in the past year you've had a new granddaughter, and your music has become the most successful part of your life. Both have probably opened your heart a little further than you've realized," said Caroline. "And both may have prepared your heart for this reunion with Erik."

"And what happens next has to come from the woman you are today, here and now, in the twenty-first century," said Diana. "Stay present, Marti."

"Just be open hearted and honest about how you feel," said Kate.

"You – you scare me to death! After tonight, you will be a *'Sadie, Sadie – married lady'!*" said Marti. "I'm not sure I will ever walk down the aisle."

"And Katie won't either, if we don't get busy! Come on in here Katie. I've got all my tools ready," said Caroline.

Caroline led Kate into a classic dressing room with a vintage dressing table, beautifully skirted in a teal moire silk. A three way mirror was mounted on the wall, along with full length mirrors to the right of it.

"How glamorous!" said Kate.

"I had a lot of extra room up here when I finally removed the rest of Frank's things, and I thought this would be the best use for the space. It gives me moments of pure femininity." Caroline put a cape around Kate's shoulders, put a shine product in her hair and began to blow it dry. She then swept it up, clamped it and drew up tendrils with soft curls that cascade from the crown to her shoulders. She excused herself from the room for a moment and returned with a basket of miniature rose buds that were affixed to tiny clamps which she then tucked in between the curls. "Since you didn't want to wear a bridal veil, I thought these might be an elegant touch. I don't think they have any fragrance that would interfere with the floral essence you're wearing. Put me on your Christmas list for that, too."

As Caroline worked on her hair, her mind was reeling with memories of the dizzying preparations for her own wedding with Frank. She struggled to stay focused, so that she might finish on schedule. As she finished, she stepped back and let Kate take a moment to get the full effect.

When Kate saw herself from all three angles, she thanked Caroline profusely. "It's beyond anything I could have ever done, Caroline. I've never worn my hair like this before – it's so...so graceful. I love it, and the tiny roses are so sweet."

Diana entered the room and added her praises. She turned the chair which put Kate's back to the mirrors and began using her own skillfulness, determined to enhance the natural beauty Kate was born with. Diana's magic makeup case had brushes of every size and shape and bottles and plastic cases that she'd purchased just for Kate, just in case Kate ever decided to wear makeup again.

Marti and Caroline entered the room to watch the *artiste* at work. They brought the dress and shoes in with them.

When Diana finished, she turned the chair around and revealed her artistry. Kate looked at herself in silence for a brief moment, then tears welled up in her eyes.

"No crying!" gasped her friends. "Breathe – just breathe," said Diana.

"All my life I've been '*a natural woman*' and never had much use for makeup, never learned and never cared enough to use it. I've loved it on all of you, but....it wasn't me. But tonight, it IS me! Thank you!"

"Let's get that gorgeous dress on you," said Marti. "We're cutting it close on our own beauty time."

Diana and Caroline left the room while Marti and Kate got dressed. Within moments, Paula and Sigrid were at the door. Caroline pulled an ice bucket with a champagne bottle in it out from behind a door.

As Kate and Marti emerged from the dressing room all eyes were a little watery. As everyone stood to cheer the bride, the corked was popped and flutes of the bubbly were passed around the room, while each told the bride how she radiant she looked.

Caroline spoke first. "I've thought about this moment over the last few months while arrangements were being made for this day, and though I could have hired people to be here to prepare Katie for this wedding and to help us all for that matter, it just didn't feel like the right thing to do. None of us are kids anymore, and a few of us have known Katie when we actually were. I wanted us to have a moment together with the bride, just us, and with all our families here this was the only time I thought we could work that out.

This marriage will be a colossal change for you, Katie, and my wish for you is that it adds dimensions of love that you never knew existed. I've grown to love Robbie almost as much as I've loved you. He is a fine man of great wisdom and character. I wish you much peace together on the road ahead."

"Okay Sadie - *almost married lady*, my thoughts go back to the beginning of our friendship. I look at the days when we had big hair and little jobs, school and budding dreams for careers... and I had a baby – then I think of your compassion. May Robbie always hold you with the same compassion you have given me and my son, and know that you are worthy of it. Then I can know this will always be a heart centered marriage," said Marti. As her voice began to crack, Sigrid stepped up.

"And I think that in the lineage of this friendship, I am next. I'll always remember when we first met. You and Marti came to pick up Erik from day care at my home. Your eyes were traveling all over my house to be sure it was a clean and safe environment for him. He would come running to you like a second mom – It was always Auntie Katie! Auntie Katie!

You were also one of my best taste testers for all my previous endeavors, and yet, as busy are you were, you always responded with a note of positive encouragement. If you can do the same with your new husband, I think you will live a long life together."

Diana lifted her glass and said, "I've only known you for a dozen or so years, but I've seen those traits in you that these women speak of, year after year. My prayer for you is that throughout your marriage to Robbie, you discover new traits about each other that deepen your love and bond you for life."

"I'm the newbie of this group, and thanks to Niki have learned from all of you, that loving friendships are essential to the gift of life itself. I wish for you and Robbie, an attentive awareness of the gifts you each bring to this marriage, and a long life together," added Paula.

As they circled the bride and raised their glasses for a toast, a faint specter of light, in the shape of a woman, barely noticeable, shown softly from the corner of the room. It radiated from its heart space, its essence of love, then slowly dissipated into nothingness.

At Last, the Wedding

"My heart to you is given: Oh, do give yours to me;
We'll lock them up together, And throw away the key."

~Frederick Saunders

A t six o'clock, Caroline was in the chapel taking in the beauty displayed before her. She was thrilled with the fabrics, the floras, the music, and the presence of the family. Surely the bride would be too nervous to see the exquisite details, she thought. She and Ric had eloped to Las Vegas to marry in Reverend Love's sanctuary of gaudiness. She married Frank in a barren little chapel in Italy, and neither wedding was an affair as elegant as this. Sometimes in the excitement of the decision to get married, the *"a .s .a p."* urge takes precedent. She asked the photographer to take several *"before"* photos, just in case weddings at the AngelFire Inn were part of her future. As Caroline turned to straighten one of the chair covers, she saw Ric enter the chapel.

"You look absolutely wonderful," he said as he awkwardly hugged her.

"You look pretty handsome yourself, Mr. Roberts," she teased as she straightened his tie and brushed off his shoulders. Both recognized this as an old habit of hers from their past together. Caroline was a bit startled by her actions. "Thank you for coming early," she said. "I'm not sure there is anything left for us to do, but I do appreciate the effort." Both turned as they heard Carmen and JB enter the chapel, arm in arm.

JB said, "I can't believe my eyes...this is amazing! I thought you said you were renting a tent!"

"What can we do to help?" said Carmen. She was dressed in a dazzling sapphire shantung short strapless dress with a cropped jacket. True to herself, she wore antique Zuni silver jewelry.

Caroline told her how stunning she looked and asked the photographer for a quick photo of the two of them together.

Ric shook hands with JB and said, "It looks like your trip was pretty remarkable. It must have taken a lot of courage to lose the ponytail. You are looking good tonight!"

"I don't think courage had anything to do with it," answered JB.

"Speaking of remarkable," said Carmen as she took Caroline aside to show off her new ring.

"Congratulations!" whispered Caroline. "Absolutely exquisite! This must account for your not showing up to toast the bride and that big smile you're wearing."

"I'll share the rest of it with you on Monday, after everyone leaves AngelFire. I can tell you however, that right now I am very grateful to the Amoroso brothers!"

Caroline returned to Ric and said, "We look rather staid in our basic black, don't we?"

"Are you kidding?" he said, "If that off-shoulder dress was in any other color, you'd be accused of upstaging the bride! I'm wearing a black suit, because – well, I wear black suits."

Caroline looked into his eyes and saw the same look she saw in them when they were in college. His hair might have turned grey, but there was the same zest for life, in those eyes. She simply smiled. *There's always something in the air at weddings,* she thought.

Camille MacArthur walked in with another musician in full regalia. She went to the front of the chapel and he stayed to the rear. She began to tune her cello, while he stayed shyly in a corner.

Within minutes Jackson and Diana Greene walked in. He was wearing a taupe colored suit with taupe shirt and violet tie. Diana was as striking as ever, in a violet suit, with a full length skirt and taupe beaded scarf. The photographer recognized the celebrity couple and asked if he might take a few photos of them. They allowed only one. Caroline and Diana walked together to the platform area to meet with Camille for a few moments.

Jackson approached Ric and said, "I'm so glad you decided to come to this."

"I'm glad she was receptive to the idea," said Ric softly. "She looks wonderful doesn't she?"

"Yes, indeed she does. She's gone to a great deal of work and expense to give these two a fine wedding. We're both happy to be a part of it. Caroline truly *believes* in marriage and she surely helped me keep mine intact. I will forever be indebted to her."

"The Amoroso brothers have helped my marriage over a bump in the road," said JB, joining Jackson and Ric. "You're gonna love these guys."

"I'm not so sure they're going to love me much. Aren't they Caroline's in-laws?" said Ric. "By the way – nice suit."

"Nice haircut, too," added Jackson.

"Thanks guys. This is the new JB, for the moment anyway... old habits are hard to break sometimes. Check in with me in a month."

"It's all about willingness, my friend, all about willingness," said Jackson. "Now I have to get in front of things here with my wife. I'll see you after the service." Jackson then joined Diana and Caroline at the dais.

Paula and all her band members arrived and took a back row. She left them alone, to come over and give Ric a hug. "I'm so glad you're here. I want you to meet my little band of musicians later at the reception.

"Brad and Jarrod will be glad to see you, too," said Ric. "You should be forewarned, they may want to sit in with the band. Both our sons play the guitar."

"They'll love it!" Paula turned to JB and said, "Wow – JB, you're looking very cool, tonight."

"I don't think anyone has ever said that to me before," said a smiling JB Robles.

The groom and his brothers arrived, in all their splendor. Robbie introduced his brothers to all those who had arrived, so far. Antonio and Giovanni each took a post at the door, and as the others began arriving, they escorted them to their seats. Both must have been charming the women all the way up the aisle, as each woman was smiling as she was seated.

Caroline made a quick call on her cell phone as soon as she saw Robbie.

Upstairs in the Inn, a nervous bride and her maid of honor were waiting. There was a knock at the door, and Marti answered it. Four year old Lilly, dressed in a long, deep purple velvet dress, was carrying a basket full of rose petals. She and her dad entered the apartment. Erik extended his arm out to Kate and said "Aunt Katie, may I be your escort to the chapel and give you away at your wedding?"

"I would be most grateful," said Kate, as she took a deep breath to keep her composure. Marti took Lilly's hand and led the way, while Erik and Kate followed. When they reached the entrance of the Inn, they were greeted by the musician who had been standing by, waiting for the bridal procession.

In the chapel, all were now present and seated. Caroline waited at the entrance with Giovanni and Antonio.

The Irish piper played his bagpipes in a traditional Irish march and led the bridal procession from the Inn to the chapel. The Celtic music echoed all the way into the chapel.

"Must be an acquired taste," whispered Antonio to his brother.

The blue cast of dusk had fallen over the entire valley. All the candles were lit, and the miniature lights strewn in the trees and along the path created an enchanting atmosphere – just as planned.

Upon the arrival of the bride, Giovanni stepped forward and extended his arm toward Marti. Caroline signaled Camille, and she began Mendelsohn's "Wedding March". Little Lilly began the promenade down the aisle spreading rose petals along the way. She stopped short at the second row where she saw her mommy and her new Papa and quickly slipped in between them for a seat.

Marti wore a classic sheath in aubergine velvet with a simple string of vintage pearls. She carried a dramatic autumnal bouquet, and for several reasons, she was simply beaming. As she and Giovanni reached the platform and took their places, all rose and watched as Erik proudly escorted the radiant bride.

Kate was luminous and her gaze was wholly fixed on Robbie. The vintage gown in ecru satin and lace perfectly complimented her pale skin and strawberry blonde hair. She carried a traditional cascading floral bouquet of ivory and honey-colored roses, green cymbidiums, with sprays of millinery pearls and ivory ribbons. As the bride stood under the chandelier, her antique pearl choker with a centerpiece cluster of amethysts caught the flickering candlelight. But nothing glistened brighter than her eyes as she walked up that aisle. When they reached the platform, Erik tenderly kissed her on her cheek, took her hand and placed it in the hand of the groom. The bride and groom then turned together and faced the two officiates.

Jackson asked all of the guests to be seated. "We have gathered here this evening for this sunset ceremony, on behalf of Katherine Mary Margaret O'Neil and Roberto Raffaele Collicci, who desire the bonds of holy matrimony. Most of us have travelled considerable distances to be here to witness this act of love and commitment. We support these two individuals who have until a year ago, lived in very different worlds. What could be more opposite than a man whose career is of high finance and a woman in a career of alternative therapies and Chinese medicine? What could they possibly have in common? The truth is...nobody cares about their careers...only their hearts, for that's where our real wisdom lies, in hearts filled with love.

As our world draws us closer and closer together, we are learning more from each other than ever before. We are transcending cultures and beliefs through the sharing of wisdom, spirituality, and love more than ever before in history. And it continues to give us all hope, as we open to that goodness of God, which dwells within each of us. May they always see this goodness in each other.

I urge you both to consider the possibility that God may have brought you together at this moment in life for the achievement of a greater purpose as a couple – greater than your individual expressions of talents and abilities. This may be a call to a love that is greater than both of you. Yes, you may be called to serve in some way you have not yet contemplated. So love each other well and travel a spiritual journey. Let us bless this union.

Diana stepped forward and said, "I have an exceptional poem that I would like to read to you from James Dillet Freeman,

> May your marriage bring you all the
> exquisite excitements a marriage should bring,
> and may life grant you also patience, tolerance,
> and understanding.
> May you need one another, but not out of weakness.
> May you want one another, but not out of lack.
> May you entice one another, but not compel one another.
> May you succeed in all important ways with one another,
> and not fail in the little graces.
> May you look for things to praise, often say,
> "I love you!" and take no notice of small faults.
> If you have quarrels that push you apart,
> may both of you hope to have good sense
> enough to take the first step back.

May you enter into the mystery which is the awareness
of one another's presence - no more physical than spiritual,
warm and near when you are side by side, and warm and near
when you are in separate rooms or even distant cities.
May you have happiness, and may you find it making one
another happy.
May you have love, and may you find it loving one another!

Now let us pray...
*"Dear God, we give thanks tonight for this beautiful gathering
of those who have come from afar to attend this celebration
of love. We realize that the bonds of your love nourish the
connectedness of each other and this our chosen family. Keep us
in your grace. Bless this man and this woman as they create a
sacred bond of marriage. Keep them in wholeness and vitality;
let their prosperity come with peace, and their love with life-long
kindness, acceptance, forgiveness and contentment. And may
they travel in an innumerable company of angels. With deepest
gratitude, we say together, Amen."*

Camille and two violinists began to play A. H. Malotte's
musical rendition of the Lord's Prayer. To everyone's delight,
Michelle Greene rose and sang a moving interpretation of the
prayer. The proud pastors were gratified.

"Katie and Robbie have opted to write their own vows, so I
would like to ask them to state them at this time. Katie, would
you begin," said Diana.

Kate handed her bouquet to Marti, turned to Robbie and
said: "Until I met you, I had begun to believe that this day
was not possible for me. I come to you in the autumn of my
life, just as I am, accepting you, just as you are. I promise
to honor and respect you and to love you wholeheartedly. I
promise to comfort you when you need it and support you in
all your endeavors. I promise to grow with you and commit
to a beautiful life together. I give you this ring, as a symbol of

love and my commitment of eternal peace between us." Kate placed a distinctive band encircled with golden laurel leaves on the third finger of his left hand.

"And Roberto, please state your vows," said Jackson.

"Katherine Mary Margaret O'Neil, from the first time I laid eyes on you, I needed to know you. My seemingly contented life has turned into one of excitement for each time we are together. I'm certain that what the future holds for us will be nothing less than miraculous. I promise to love you with passion and compassion, to fervently bring our two worlds together and seek to discover new pathways for us, as partners side by side. I pledge in front of my brothers and our friends to cherish you with all my heart. I give you this ring as a symbol of timeless, unending love." And he placed a distinctive band encircled with golden laurel leaves centered with a trillion cut diamond, on the third finger on her left hand.

Jackson asked "Roberto, do you take Katherine to be your lawfully wedded wife?"

"I do."

Diana asked, "Katherine, do you take Roberto to be your lawfully wedded husband?"

Kate opened her mouth, but nothing came out. She tried a second time, but again was voiceless. Jackson and Diana remained silent. Diana quickly glared at Marti, who glared at Caroline, who glared at Julia, then Sigrid, who glared right back to Caroline, who then of course glared back at Marti.

Robbie pulled her forward and kissed her deeply, passionately. When he stepped back from her, Kate took a breath and said exuberantly, "Forever and ever, I do!"

"Okay then – we both pronounce you, husband and wife!" said Jackson and Diana in unison.

"Would you like to kiss the bride again?" asked Jackson.

Without the need to answer, Robbie pulled Kate toward him and kissed her tenderly. With applause, a little relief and good wishes, all attendees cheered. The groom escorted the bride back down the aisle and Giovanni and Marti followed. They stepped outside for a moment and Giovanni hugged his brother and said, "I'm truly happy for you, Robbie. That was one scary moment there, brother. I almost thought she changed her mind."

Marti hugged the bride and Kate whispered, "That was just the most important question of my entire life, and I lost myself for a hot second. But my heart knew exactly what I wanted."

The Reception

"When two people find selfless love in this world, it does call for a toast!"

- Simran Khurana

*T*he intimate group of friends and families extended their heart-felt congratulations and began a procession on the now moonlit walkway, under a thousand stars, toward the APAC building for the reception. Caroline and the wedding party stayed behind in the chapel for more photography. Carmen and JB would host the reception until they all arrived, which technically meant the bar was open.

There was little that was recognizable as the AngelFire Performing Arts Center. Crews had transformed the room into starlit night at an elegant cabaret. Caroline had removed all the original seating and replaced it with a parquet dance floor. Opposite the stage was the head table, with eight tables for two on the right and eight more tables for two on the left forming a crescent around the dance floor. All the closely-spaced tables were glowing in candlelight and a low autumnal floral arrangements extending to the tables edge, gave the illusion of one grand dining table. A large iron and crystal chandelier was centered over the dance floor and a smaller one hung off-centered over the stage. Potted trees with twinkling lights defined the corners of the room. Most of the room had been draped, and a section was cordoned off with black dividers, behind which the caterers and wait staff worked furiously.

As the wedding party arrived, they were escorted to their seats, as were the guests, so there would be no delay in serving the dinner. Eighteen waiters carrying ice buckets with bottles of champagne came from behind the curtained staging area and stood behind each of the tables. Two waiters were designated for the head table. In perfect synchronization – Corks were popped and the bubbling toasts began!

Camille and two violinists took the moment as a signal to begin playing the dinner music. The young musicians had coordinated a rotation whereby two by two they would each play during dinner, so each would miss very little of the food. Paula was proud of both their performance and their behavior.

All eighteen waiters disappeared and reappeared with trays of

"Mixed Aperitifs with Canapés di Antipasti".

The bride leaned over to Marti and said, "This all looks fabulous, but I'm not sure I could eat a thing!"

"With all the toasting that will happen tonight, you ought to consider eating more – not less," said Marti. She raised her glass and nodded to her son Erik. Laney had managed to squeeze a high chair into the configuration for baby Lisa. Seated at the table next to them was their sweet little flower girl Lilly and her Papa Erik, Sr., who also raised his glass with a wink toward Marti.

Erik was pleased to have Arturo sitting to his right and the attractive Sigrid directly across the table. Arturo and Erik had the distinction of being welcome newcomers to this chosen family. Both had exchanged comments over the weekend regarding this close-knit, yet open-hearted group. "I understand you're the artist who created the wedding cake," said Erik. "How on earth did you get it all the way up here?"

"Very carefully," answered Arturo. "Actually, I did the baking and some of the decorating at a friend's place in Santa Fe. Sigrid and I assembled most of it in her bungalow."

"It really is a work of art and I love Chef Niccolini's display for it, too" said Sigrid. "It's a wonderful presentation. I just hope that spotlight doesn't create any heat and melt any of the flowers."

"When do we get to eat the cake?" asked Jenny, who was seated at the next table with her sister Mattie.

"I'll get you some cake as soon as they cut it," said Jarrod, who was happily sitting with Sherri at the next table.

The eighteen waiters reappeared, lined up behind each table, and again with orchestrated service, lifted the covers from their trays and next revealed...

"Smoked Mozzarella and Pumpkin Raviolis"

"It's a good thing these portions are small," said Sherri. "We would be rolling our way back to our rooms."

"I'm guessing these portions are small, because there is much more to come," said Jarrod. "We may just have to work it off on the dance floor."

"That works just fine for me," said Brad, at the next table and sitting across from Lauren Greene, who added, "You know how much I love to dance, Brad. Remember your mother dragging you to my dance recitals when we were little kids?"

"I thought you were a star," said Brad. "And now you're with the Houston Ballet? You don't just love to dance, you *live* to dance!"

"We hope you like our dance music," said the two young musicians at the next table.

"Which one of you plays the guitar?" asked Brad.

"Jorge does – he's at the next table."

"Do you think I might be able to join you later?" asked Brad, leaning forward to find Jorge.

"If Ms. Paula says it's okay," said Jorge. "Are you any good?"

As traditions were remembered, glasses were clinked and the bride and groom kissed.

"Hey little brother, who's your chef tonight?" asked Giovanni.

"Niccolini," said Robbie.

"*Our* Bobbie Niccolini? How did you get him to come up here?"

"Frankie brought him up here once. Caroline used him for a dinner last year and everyone liked him, so she hired him to be on staff."

"It is a small, small world. I'll say hello to him later. So, will you be too embarrassed if I dance with the women here tonight?" asked Giovanni.

"Is there any particular woman you have your eye on tonight, Gio?" asked Robbie.

"I intend to dance with each and every one of them, Robbie," said Giovanni. "I have a reputation to keep up and this is a beautiful crowd. Are any of these women single?"

"Single, yes - available, probably not," said Robbie.

"My brother is quite the dancer," said Antonio who was sitting to Giovanni's left, and across from Michelle Greene, who had become his dinner partner. "He took ballroom dancing classes in his younger days."

"Then he will have to find my sister Lauren, who is the dancer in our family," said Michelle.

"Your mother is a fine dancer too, as I recall," added Jackson, who was sitting to Antonio's left and directly across from Diana, who was pleased to be sitting close enough to their daughter and Antonio to eavesdrop on their conversations.

"At least one of your children chose to sit near you for this dinner," said Ric, who was sitting to Jackson's left. Caroline had not yet joined him at their table. "My boys chose to be on the other side of the room tonight."

"Oh, they just want to have fun," said David, who was sitting to Ric's left. Julia of course was directly across from him, intending to sit next to Caroline.

"I think everyone will have fun tonight," said JB as he looked adoringly across the table at his wife.

Paula and Camille sat at the next table, but were so focused on their students, they had barely eaten or joined in on much of the conversation. When Camille left to take another turn on stage, Carmen leaned over toward Paula and whispered, "She is an absolute work of art!"

"She is – you're right. Camille is wonderful with the kids, too. She's also very dedicated to her music...it's her life," said Paula.

"I think we can say the same about you," said Carmen. "I'm guessing it's your *entire* life."

"I think that's what happens when we do what we love most, we end up making it our complete lives. I'm guessing Lauren Greene's life is all about dance and look at Caroline, her life is all about AngelFire."

The procession of waiters arrived to make their next grand presentation....

"Grilled Sea Bass with Lemon Sauce ~ Risotto with Herbs and Vegetables"
Paired with a Pinot Grigio

Caroline joined the family just as her entrée was placed. "We took a vote," she said to Julia. "We pored over several menus and I let the staff vote – with a great deal of taste-testing and a lot of fun."

"You're fortunate that the chef is an agreeable sort," said Julia.

"I assume he provided you with the assortment of menus," said Ric.

"Exactly," said Caroline.

"So far, it has been delectable, and if you will look around it appears that everyone agrees," added Ric. "I hope this means you can relax now."

Caroline took a moment to look around and take in the palpable joy of all the families in communion with their laughter and affection. The music, the cuisine, the ambiance and having her own family with her, created the happiest moments she had felt in at least two years. In that very moment, all she could feel was gratitude.

As the entrées were finished the waiters returned and presented in typical Italian fashion...

"Insalata Capricciosa"
Fresh Greens, Sliced Celeste Figs & Pears, Shaved
Parmigianino

When it looked as if all were nearly finished with their salads, Giovanni rose to give a toast to his brother, "Good evening everyone. I would like ask you to raise a glass to my brother, the groom. Robbie has, for his whole life been a man who keeps his head and wits about him, and he was always, even as a kid, a *wholelotta* smart and the one who was the rock. Suddenly, about a year ago, he lost his heart – to the woman who became his bride tonight. Katie has captured his heart and all his love. She comes from a completely different world than his and she brings to him another kind of love. Oh – and she's *a wholelotta* smart, too."

Looking directly at Robbie, he said, "I've already seen how you've become part of a new family, a good family, and we invite you to make Katie part of our family, too. On behalf of my bothers Sal and Antonio, we're truly thrilled for you Robbie, and we wish you and Katie lifelong happiness."

The crowd raised their glasses to Robbie and Kate and cheered the couple with champagne and applause.

It was then Marti's turn to give her toast to the bride. She rose and said, "I have known Katie my whole adult life, and to me she is the symbol of kindness. I was with her when she was introduced to Robbie, by Caroline, a little over a year ago at a restaurant in Santa Fe. When he walked away, she asked Caroline, *"Who is that darling man?"* She was smitten. I hardly recognized Katie, as she was so immediately fascinated by this man." Marti looked Kate directly in the eye and said, "Now you've done it – you've married this darling man. And no one could be happier for you than I am tonight, except maybe this room full of family and friends, who join me in wishing you the kind of love you deserve; the same gentle compassionate and heart-centered thoughtfulness that you have shown to all of us. For the rest of your life, may you and Robbie live in the benevolence of our Creator, may you each enjoy brilliant health and joyous love." Marti's voice started to crack and Kate rose, gave her a hug and thanked her with a whisper.

Glasses were raised again, and the circle of AngelFire women all said aloud, "We love you Katie!"

All the musicians had assembled on the stage while the speakers were making their speeches. They were wide eyed, grinning broadly and ready to show what they could do. The first to speak was Paula who asked, "Are we ready for a little dancing, tonight?" and she gave her cue to the drummer, who started the first beat. With great jubilation, the dance floor filled up quickly.

Giovanni was first to leave the bride's table, and afterward Marti left to join Erik. Lilly had found her way to Sherri's girls, who were already dancing. Marti took Lisa out of her high chair, but could barely keep her still on her lap. "She may not walk yet, but she might start dancing tonight! She sure loves the music," said Marti, juggling the baby on her lap. "Erik, you and Laney better grab the moment to dance while she's willing to be on my lap."

"Don't worry mom. We'll be having a great time. I'll be taking her upstairs and putting her to bed in a few minutes. Carmen arranged for babysitters for the girls. Lilly, Mattie and Jenny are going to upstairs and watch a Disney movie with one of the housekeeping staff," said Laney.

"That Carmen thinks of everything!" said Marti.

"Good! That means that you and I can have a good time, too," said Erik, Sr., which made Marti smile.

It was no surprise to JB that the Amoroso brothers would want to dance with every woman in the room. Giovanni's first choice was to dance with Carmen, who willingly accepted his invitation.

After a few swirls and twirls on the dance floor Carmen spoke to Giovanni. "My husband said you are the one who is responsible for his new haircut," she said, as he placed his hand on her upper back and gently lowered her backward. Equally as gentle, was the way he returned her to a fully upright position and twirled her softly to the right.

"I am innocent," he said. "Do you like to Tango?"

"I'm sorry. I don't do the ballroom dances," said Carmen. "But I'm sure there are a few women here who can keep up with you."

"Your husband repeatedly told us of your beauty, but his words did not adequately describe your loveliness," he sighed. He gently dipped and twirled her around the dance floor and made her look as if she knew exactly what she was doing.

"Oh my God - you *are* everything he told me about you," laughed Carmen. "May I ask you a personal question?"

"Do I have to answer it?" asked Giovanni.

"Not if you don't want to." Twirl, five, six, seven, eight...

"Have you ever been married?" asked Carmen.

"Of course I have been married," answered Giovanni. "Many times." As the music stopped, he took her hand and led her back to the table and her smiling husband.

"My turn," said JB, not allowing his wife to be seated. He took her by the hand and led her back to the dance floor. "We're not working tonight. Let's just enjoy the evening."

Who are you? thought Carmen.

Antonio opened his dance card with the choice of a dance with Diana. "Reverend, may I have this dance?"

"I'd be delighted!" said Diana as she took Antonio's arm and moved around the dance floor like they had been dance partners in a previous life. Jackson and Michelle decided to join them. Michelle glared at her mother as if to say *who are you?*

Erik and Laney returned to the Inn to get the girls settled in for the night. His parents took an awkward step forward and danced together for the first time since their youth. The icy interior of Marti Westerlund was beginning to melt. *Not now* – she told herself – *not now.* She was in the arms of the only man she had ever truly loved. Her mind told her that their love once was real, but that it had taken place a very long time ago. Her heart said something else. *Oh God*, she thought.

The bride and groom moved from table to table in gratitude to each person for their efforts in attending this destination wedding. Robbie only knew a handful of their names and who was related to whom. Her chosen family would become his chosen family, and he would make sure his contributions to this family, mattered.

Paula spoke, introducing the band members and stating a few words about the ABQ Youth Orchestra, which drew abundant applause. When the applause diminished, she said "We have created a wonderful program for the Youth Orchestra this year, using a Lennon- McCartney theme. I've been working on a song in memory of Nicole Roberts that I love and think you might enjoy. Would you like to hear it?"

Oh no! thought Caroline, as she began to move toward the stage, trying to get Paula's attention. *Everyone will start crying! What is she thinking?* She was too late...

Paula called out, "One... two... three...four!"

Well she was just seventeen, And you know what I mean
And the way she looked Was way beyond compare
So how could I dance with another, Ooo, when I saw her standing there?
Well she looked at me And I, I could see, That before too long I'd fall in love with her
She wouldn't dance with another Woo, when I saw her standing there
Well my heart went boom When I crossed that room And I held her hand in mine
Oh, we danced through the night And we held each other tight

And before too long, I fell in love with her
Now I'll never dance with another Woo, since I saw her
standing there
Well we danced through the night And we held each other tight
And before too long I fell in love with her
Now I'll never dance with another Ooo, since I saw her
standing there

The crowd sang along, and the band rocked on...and Caroline did, too.

By the time the song ended, Giovanni had asked Caroline to dance with him. It was a pure pleasure to dance with a man who simply glided across the floor.

"You've created a memorable wedding for Robbie and Katie tonight; every part of it was beautiful, just beautiful," said Giovanni. "The truth is, I never got this whole mountain living thing that Frankie loved so much. I know that this weekend is an exception, but I'm seeing the beauty of it for the first time. I'm sorry we didn't visit more when Frankie was alive."

"Thank you Gio. I'm glad you're enjoying yourself," said Caroline. "I'm' sorry Sal was unable to join us tonight."

"Salie is all business...almost like Robbie. But I'm not so sure Robbie will stay '*all business*' anymore. Marrying Kate may have just changed everything."

"That's funny. I usually think of Kate as all business. She has been completely devoted to her clinic for many years. I was hoping that Robbie would change some of that for her. Well, I guess we will see what love does for both of them," said Caroline.

"I know we don't know each other very well, and I'm certain that Frankie left you financially strong, but if you ever need anything – we would like to be there for you. My brothers and I regret that we never got to know you. Frankie used to say that you were here as part of his dream life. At least we always knew he lived a happy life."

"We were happy, Gio...very happy. Now I think it is time for me to get the cake. Why don't you dance with my sister Julia? She *loves* ballroom dancing." Caroline walked away from Giovanni with a lump in her throat.

Within minutes the staff rolled out a fully skirted table with the delicate wedding cake and centered it in front of the brides table. Robbie and Kate first gave credit to the artistic talents of Arturo Montecito for his exquisite creation. Arturo humbly bowed his head at the table, without standing for the applause. The photographer caught Kate and Robbie make the first slice on camera, then the professionals took over and each piece of the delightful cake was plated and served with a hand painted chocolate flower on the side.

And on the other side of the room...Sherri said, "Mom...I just can't stop looking at you. I'm sorry if I am being rude; this is all so unreal. I haven't seen you in a while, but..." started Sherri.

"Sherri, it's been a very long while. Too long for a grandma to be away from her granddaughters," said Sigrid. "Your brothers live on the other side of the country, and I see them and my grandsons only once a year. I hope I can spend more time with the girls."

"You may get your wish. There's something I haven't told you yet," said Sherri.

"Is that Julia dancing cheek to cheek with the best man?" asked Sigrid. "Hmmm."

"Mother, I'm trying to tell you something."

"I already know."

"Have you been talking to Jarrod, because I haven't," started Sherri. She turned and glared at Jarrod, who responded by throwing his hands up and shrugging his shoulders.

"I swear, I said nothing!" said Jarrod.

"Stop," said Sigrid. "Artie and I were out for dinner one night and we ran into Michael. We had a drink together, and he told me where things are with you two."

"He did? Wow, I'm shocked. He's always so private and unwilling to share anything too personal," said Sherri. "Wait... that can only mean one thing. He was with someone, and he didn't want you to think he was cheating on me. I'm right, aren't I?"

"Well, actually we were leaving the restaurant and he was just coming in," said Artie, who thought it best to avoid any further drama. He rose from the table and asked Jenny and Mattie, "Would either of you two young ladies like to dance before you go upstairs for your movie?"

"Me!" said Jenny.

"No - me!" said Mattie.

"I think I can dance with both of you at the same time – let's give it a try, shall we?" Both girls joined Arturo as he moved them out of hearing distance from their mother and Sigrid.

"Is he always this thoughtful?" asked Sherri.

"So far," said Sigrid. "I figure we have less than four minutes to have this conversation, which we should have had months ago. So tell me what's going on with you and why you came here this weekend."

"Okay, I'm trying to work on myself. Since Michael left, I've been in therapy, and I have a 'to do list' which includes making amends with you. I know I owe you apologies for many things," said Sherri.

"Many, many things," added Sigrid.

"Mother - I had a little speech prepared and in my egoist brain. I thought you were alone and suffering because of all the pain I've caused you, but you seem to be doing way better, without me in your life. So I'm not clear on what I should be saying. Regardless, I *am* sorry...and I'm incredibly happy for you. I am happy about your success with the bakery and pleased about your relationship with Artie. He's a lucky man and you deserve to have some fun for a change."

"Thank you, Sherri." Mother and daughter leaned in and hugged each other.

"So what else is on this 'to do list' of yours?" asked Sigrid.

"A few more apologies, and well, it looks like I may have to find a job. I haven't worked since Mattie was born, so that may mean an entry level position somewhere."

"Wow! That *is* Julia dancing cheek to cheek with the best man!" said Sigrid. "Sorry honey, this is too much of a celebration for us to be so serious tonight. I don't want you to worry about anything."

"Why? Do you have something in mind?" asked Sherri.

"Maybe - Maybe not. We're working on a project that may provide just the right job for you," said Sigrid.

Artie returned to the table with two very happy little girls. He turned to Sigrid and said, "May I have this dance, beautiful lady?"

To which she replied, "por supuesto, mi amor!"

"We understood you grandma!" said Mattie and Jenny.

"Okay, how about if uncle Jarrod takes you two ladies upstairs at the Inn to join Lilly for a movie?"

"Yeah!' said Jenny.

"I don't want to," said Mattie.

"Then there will be no balloon ride with us tomorrow morning because you'll be too tired, and I guess we'll have to leave you behind to sleep in. Okay, see ya!" said Jarrod.

"Balloon rides?" said Sherri, Mattie and Jenny in unison. "Yes! I'll go now," said Mattie.

"I'll be back in a few minutes, Sherri. Save me a dance or two, or three, or four..." said Jarrod as he walked away with Jenny and Mattie.

Antonio was heading toward Lauren Greene when he saw Sherri sitting alone, so he asked, "May I have this dance, lovely lady?" This was not a ballad and between the two of them there was a *"wholelotta shakin' goin' on!"* Brad and Lauren joined in and the girls seemed to have a bit of a competition. Diana turned to Jackson and said "So much for our little ballerina."

Erik and Marti, were oblivious and Ric leaned over to Jackson and said," Back in the day, that would have been our wives!"

"I heard that," said Caroline as she approached Ric and the Greenes. "These kids dance very differently than we did."

"No they don't," said David. "With the exception of my wife maybe. Aaaand there goes Julia, dancing cheek to cheek with the best man, again. Thank you God, for the best man, I won't have to be cha-cha-ing, tango-ing or rhumba-ing through the night. I'll wait for a slower tempo and we'll do a little fox trot and Julia will be happy."

"She's already looking pretty happy," said Caroline.

Brad noticed Jarrod returning to the reception and asked Antonio to switch partners with him. Neither Sherri nor Lauren cared as both were enjoying the great music. When Jarrod joined them on the dance floor, he then partnered with Sherri. Brad made his exit and found his dad.

"I saw that move, son. You're a good brother," said Ric.

I saw that too. Brad, you're a good man," said Jackson.

"Hey, I just wanted to dance with Michelle, and so I handed Sherri off to Jarrod!" said Brad.

Ric turned to Jackson and said, "It's over; we know nothing."

As Caroline drew near, Ric took the opportunity to ask her to dance.

"I think I'd like that, I can't remember the last time I danced with you."

"I don't mind telling you that this weekend has been both fascinating and complicated for me," said Ric. "I'm fascinated by how you've created quite another life for yourself at AngelFire. You've produced this elegant affair in a region that has few resources. Look around, everyone is having a wonderful time."

"And there's not a politician in sight...and I think you're enjoying yourself, too," said Caroline. "Is that what's complicated for you, Ric?"

"No politicians? No, that doesn't seem to be an issue for me. Complicated? Yes, on many levels. Caroline, this may not be an appropriate time, but may I ask you why Sal Amoroso didn't come to the wedding?" asked Ric.

"I think Robbie said he had to stay in Las Vegas for business reasons. Why do you ask?" said Caroline.

"I'm asking, because if any of your money is tied to the Amoroso businesses, you may want to start moving some of it. There's an investigation pending that may or may not be a problem."

"That's interesting...Robbie's been moving money for the past month," said Caroline. "I don't want to know how you know this – or if you should have even told me about it."

"No doubt you're protected," said Ric.

"Right," said Caroline. "So what else is so complicated?"

"For one thing, Paula's resemblance to Nicole can be disarming, from time to time, yet the biggest complication–well, it's you. I have some great memories of Caroline Roberts, but you're definitely not her anymore. You are actually much more than she was. You're a successful business woman now, and you seem to have become a sort of matriarchal figure for this gathering of people we love. I think I would like to get to know this Caroline better. Is that a possibility?"

"To be truthful, I've noticed a few changes in you, too. Besides the fact that there is no phone attached to your ear and you don't seem to need to be going ninety miles an hour all day, I've seen how you are with our sons, and our friends, and Julia, too. I heard you had a lovely day with her and David, yesterday. She was impressed."

"That was nice of her," said Ric. "Frankly, I never thought she liked me very much."

"We have all mellowed with age, don't you agree? Most of all, I don't think I told you this, but I was deeply moved by how you handled everything with Nicole. I saw a level of tenderness in you I hadn't seen in a very long time."

"How kind. Thank you, Caroline. This is too much of a celebration for us to travel down that road. We can talk more about that tomorrow," said Ric. "You didn't answer my question."

"What question?" said Caroline.

"I was hoping to come up with something brilliant. Something that would make you and I spend some time together. I'd like to get to know Caroline Amoroso. I just want to see if there is anything...or that there could be anything, or..."

Before Caroline could answer his question, Carmen interrupted them and said, "Uh, guys...the music stopped."

"Are you having a good time?" Robbie asked his brothers. "I think I've seen you two dance with nearly every woman in the room."

"Everyone but the blonde over there in the red dress. She's glued to the baker guy who made the cake," said Antonio.

"I at least got to dance with her hot daughter," said Giovanni.

"Gio, you seem to have enjoyed Caroline's sister, Julia," said Robbie.

"Yes, and I can't wait to see the bruises on my shins from her tango kicks, but other than that, she's a great dancer. I called our driver, Robbie. We have the keys to the condo, so if you don't mind we'll say goodnight to everyone. We have a plane to catch tomorrow morning." Robbie thanked his brothers for everything and watched them make the rounds in the room. They were both real gentlemen tonight, and he was grateful.

When the band returned from their break, Paula asked if any of the talented musicians and singers of the family wanted to sit in with the band. Brad was the first to grab his bass guitar and join in, but the bigger surprise came when his dad, Ric, took Paula's guitar. Between the two of them, they rocked the house.

Paula asked Marti if she would be so gracious as to share her award winning talents and play something special for the bride and groom. Reluctantly, Marti went to the stage.

Erik leaned toward his dad and said, "I think I know exactly what she'll play. I'm guessing this will be my Aunt Katie's favorite piece."

Caroline and Diana looked at each other with the same thought.

A note of seriousness washed over Marti's face. Then, with a side wink to Paula, she hit the keyboard and broke out in song...

> *You shake my nerves and you rattle my brain*
> *Too much love drives a girl insane*
> *You broke my will*
> *But what a thrill*
> *Goodness gracious great balls of fire!*

I laughed at love cause I thought it was funny
But you came along and moooooved me honey
I've changed my mind
This love is fine
Goodness gracious great balls of fire!

With screams of laughter the rest of the crowd sang along...
Kiss me baby
Mmmm feels good
Hold me baby
Well I want to love you like a lover should
You're fine, so kind
Got to tell this world that you're mine mine mine mine
I chew my nails and I twiddle my thumbs
I'm real nervous but it sure is fun
C'mon baby, you drive me crazy
Goodness gracious great balls of fire!

And the band played on, until the hour became late. Robbie and Katie bid farewell to all as they were boarding a plane for San Francisco, early in the morning. Once there, they would be catching a flight for a tour of the Far East – no doubt the bride's choice for the honeymoon.

The Greenes were still on east coast time and were the first of the circle of friends to leave. Julia was now without a dance partner and David had done his foxtrot duty, so they were both ready to call it a night. Marti and Erik had slipped away without saying goodnight. Sigrid and Arturo had been enjoying the crowd but were essentially in a world of their own. The younger generation was still on the dance floor.

Caroline and Carmen were behind the curtained staging area, distributing checks to the catering staff. Chef Niccolini had fulfilled all their requests and exceeded their expectations. Caroline provided him with a generous bonus.

"Well, we did it," said Caroline to Carmen. "I think it all turned out pretty much the way we planned it."

"Nothing about this evening with my husband was the way I planned it," said Carmen. "Did you see him tonight?"

"He danced with Marti, Siggy, Diana, and Kate!"

"JB didn't dance with me," said Caroline.

"That's because I finally got him to stick to dancing with his wife," said Carmen. "I guess he thinks he's an Amoroso now."

"Take him home Mrs. Robles – Good night!" said Caroline. She stayed in the back of the room as Paula called out the last dance. From a distance, Paula's uncanny resemblance to Nicole was a reminder of who was missing at this joyous occasion. Yet Caroline knew better than anyone that sometimes those who have gone before us are just a breath away.

After the Ball is Over...

"After the ball was over, after the break of morn, After the dancers'
leaving, after the stars are gone;"

— Charles K. Harris, 1891

*E*ventually, after organizing the collection of instruments and musicians, Paula made her way to the back of the room. Caroline presented Paula with an envelope of checks for each of the musicians and an additional contribution for the Youth Orchestra.

"Camille and your band surpassed all our expectations," said Caroline. "I hope your young musicians enjoyed the party, too."

"They had a blast! They're all pretty wired up about it. I just hope they will sleep tonight," said Paula.

Camille and the band approached them and Jorge spoke for them all, "Missus Amoroso, we all want to thank you for the opportunity to attend this beautiful wedding, have the big dinner, and play our music for your family. We will not forget this and we hope you will remember us for the next time."

"Next time - *If there is a next time*...I will definitely call for you," said Caroline.

After all the goodnights and goodbyes were said, Caroline heard someone approaching from behind. It was Ric.

"Look what I found," he said holding two wine glasses and an unopened bottle of wine. "May I pour you a glass?"

"Sure, why not," said Caroline. "I missed out on most of the toasting tonight."

"You must be happy with the way everything turned out," he said.

"I am very pleased, and I'm so glad our sons came up for this. It's hard for me to get either of them up here for a visit. I usually have to go to California to see them," said Caroline.

"I'm afraid I have to do the same. They want little to do with Washington," said Ric.

"I need to close this room up for the night. The staff will be coming back in the morning to start taking it all apart. Why don't you bring that wine and we'll finish talking at the Inn. I'm sure there is a wonderful fire in the great room."

Ric and Caroline stopped on the walkway back to the Inn to take in the stars. "What a spectacular night," said Ric.

"Nature is glorious up here at any hour...and peaceful," added Caroline. As they approached the bungalows, she noticed that the lights were on at "Annie Oakley's", a.k.a. Marti's place.

"I guess she can't sleep," said Caroline. Ric said nothing, but responded with a smile. They entered the Inn and left the door unlocked. The fire in the great room was roaring and they pulled two large leather club chairs over to face the fire. They heard laughter above and decided that the Greene girls, Sherri, and their sons were all together, enjoying the last of the night.

"Are you still happy here at AngelFire, Caroline?"

"I would say I'm content, for now anyway. I haven't figured out if this is it for me, or if there is something else I should be doing. I am more than comfortable and I have the freedom to do anything I want to do, so I will be honest and tell you I'm perplexed, to say the least."

"I'm glad. There *is* more for you to do, Caroline. There is always more to do, for those of us who care. We're just getting wiser...and *God forgive me for saying this* – older. We have a different perspective now about *changing the world* versus *making a difference*. You do not have to work....so I recommend that you wait for '*the call*'."

"The Call?" she asked.

"That's right. When you get a call to do something important, you'll know it and you will respond to it accordingly. That's who you are, and this I do know to be true."

And in this very moment the only sound was the crackling of the fire.

Doors

"Once my heart was captured, reason was shown the door..."

George Sand

The morning air was fresh, clear and bright, crisp and cool. It was a perfect day for hot air ballooning. It called for an early morning in the dining room at the AngelFire Inn, which was abuzz with excitement. The coffee was flowing and the added attraction of caramel apple waffles were a big hit. But only the younger generation and the children were present. All parents were yet unaccounted for.

Carmen and JB were first of their peers to cheerfully join the group. Carmen welcomed everyone and announced that the balloon rides would begin within the hour, as the balloonists had arrived and were in the process of inflating their giant balloons. She reminded everyone to bring their cameras and extra sweaters or jackets, and scarves. The AngelFire vans would take them by groups of six out to the launch site.

JB also suggested that the horses would be available for riding for those who might not want to go ballooning. He invited the children to come out to the corral to see the new foal they had been raising since the Spring. "This new horse is still looking for a name," said JB, "Maybe one of the girls can help us with that." The idea of naming a horse brought a rise of chatter from the children's table.

"Perfect," said Sherri, "I think we'll go name a horse today. I'm not sure my stomach could handle hot air ballooning. I'm getting woozy just thinking about it. Besides, I'm not sure I want to be in the room when my mother and her – uh, Artie walk in together."

"I'll take the girls up for a balloon ride. I promised them last night, remember?" said Jarrod.

"You're a peach, Jarrod. I don't know how this weekend would've turned out without you," said Sherri. Jarrod beamed and said, "I'll go tell the girls we'd better get started and head for the corral."

Sherri turned to Erik and Brad and asked, "Why are you two so quiet this morning?" Laney was returning from the buffet table with more coffee. Erik had his head in his hands, and Brad had barely touched his food.

"I don't think my dad came back to his room last night," mumbled Erik.

"My dad's been sharing a room with me, and he didn't come back either," said Brad, looking like he'd just lost his dog.

"So you think your parents were together? *Like – together, together?* Oh my – " started Sherri.

"STOP – right there, all three of you," said Laney. She stood by her chair and said, "The three of you listen up – because I am only going to say this once. I've got two things to say. One – This is LIFE – their life, and you have no idea what did or did not happen last night. It just goes to show you that even at their age, it never stops. We're all just trying to work out our lives. Can you understand that? And – Two" – she snapped her fingers – "IT IS NONE" - she snapped her fingers again – "OF YOUR BUSINESS!" –

she snapped her fingers a third time – leaving the mark of Zorro in the air." Laney grabbed her coffee and started to leave the table, then turned back to her husband and said, "Go take your daughters out to see the horses."

"I think I'll go with you," said Brad. Sherri obediently joined them.

Just as the dining room was clearing out, Julia and David walked in. David went directly to the buffet table. Carmen rose and greeted them. Laney was now sitting with Lauren and Michelle Greene.

"Best wedding I've been to in a very long time," said Julia. "Are the bride and groom gone already? We didn't hear a thing."

"They had to be in Santa Fe this morning to catch a flight," answered Carmen. "I have no idea what time they left."

"Good morning everybody!" said Caroline. She had obviously been up for some time and seemed fresh and with no '*morning after*' look, at all.

"I thought you'd be exhausted this morning," said Julia. "You look great! It was a wonderful wedding, Caroline."

"I was glad to see you enjoying yourself last night," said Caroline.

David returned to the table and said, "I've already packed the car. We'll be leaving after breakfast. We've both had an enjoyable weekend here at AngelFire, Caroline, and I hope that you will come to Santa Barbara again, soon. We're hosting Thanksgiving this year and we'd love it if you and the boys would join us."

"Thank you David. I would like that. I'll see what I can co-ordinate with them. It always depends on the snow up here."

"Except that '*we have people for that*' now," added Carmen as she walked up and joined the conversation.

"Good morning everyone," said Jackson and Diana Greene in unison. Diana hugged Julia, Caroline, and Carmen, while Jackson headed straight for the buffet table. He returned quickly with two cups of coffee. "We're all packed and will be leaving for Santa Fe as soon as the girls have their balloon rides," said Diana

"You're not going up?" asked Carmen.

"I believe that would fall under the reckless endangerment clause in our contracts," said Jackson. "But Lauren and Michelle are welcome to go up if they wish."

"We're going, dad. Don't you know that ballooning is the safest and oldest form of flight?" said Michelle. The Greenes went to the breakfast buffet and then joined their daughters.

There was no mistaking the laughter now heard from the entry way, was that of Sigrid. It seemed that Arturo was quite the comic. They entered and brought their jovial vitality into the room which evoked smiles from the others and the tiniest hint of raised eyebrows as Marti and Erik walked in together behind them.

"Okay, you have to share. What's so funny?" said Carmen.

And from the other end of the room, came the answer. "Life," said Ric, as he entered the room from the staircase. "Life is funny, and where are our kids?"

"They're out looking at the horses with the little ones. JB asked them to name the new foal," said Carmen. *And in avoidance of this scene,* she thought. Carmen's cell phone was buzzing with a text message, indicating that the van was ready to take the first group out to the launch site. Carmen asked which six people would like to go on the first ride.

Diana rose from her chair and walked over to Caroline and said, "I think that you and I, and Carmen, Sigrid, Marti and Julia, should take the first ride."

"But I wasn't planning to go," said Julia. "We're leaving for the Grand Canyon this morning."

"Let's just do it!" said Carmen.

And much to the surprise of Jackson, David, Erik, Ric and Arturo, the six women left the building.

JB walked in as they were leaving and said, "And there they go...*The Women of AngelFire.* I guess they need to spend a little time together this morning."

"I'm sure they have a lot to talk about," said David. "Hey, did they name the horse?"

"Yes, they called it – *Spirit*"

In the van, Julia commented on her sister's seemingly inexhaustible energy.

"Well – *Miss Ginger Rogers*, with all the dancing you did last night, I thought you'd be the one who'd be exhausted this morning," said Caroline.

"I don't know what you're talking about," answered Julia.

"It looked to me like you caught the eye of the Best Man last night," said Diana.

Julia laughed and said, "Siggy's the one with the handsome young man. Handsome young men are not attracted to me anymore. They are attracted to my daughter, and some openly to my son. I look at them all and ask myself when did this happen? What was I doing when my youth slipped away? I don't feel old. Yet, when I look into the mirror, I ask – who the hell are you? The future looks so vague, these days. I need to make it look like autumn in these mountains."

"I seem to recall that you moved around that dance floor like a twenty-something, last night! That ought to put a little glow in your cheeks," said Caroline.

A ten minute ride to the launch site and a ten minute safety orientation before boarding, and suddenly, they were up and away from everything and everyone.

"What a spectacular way to end this year's gathering," said Diana. "Just look at this!"

"So peaceful," said Caroline. "That's what I love the most."

"Takes my breath away," added Marti.

"Actually, you took my breath away this morning, walking in with Erik," said Caroline. "Perhaps we've opened another door?"

"*The truth shall set you free*....is what you all said last year. Now that the truth is out, I feel like I'm standing at a door all right, and have no idea what is on the other side of it," said Marti.

"Marti, is that door open or closed?" asked Diana. "Remember, this is the door to your heart."

"I understand, Marti. I seem to be opening and closing that door a lot lately, myself. I know I am as scared as a kid in a haunted house," said Sigrid. "But I am having fun!"

"When I left last night, you were still with Ric," said Carmen to Caroline. "How's that door to your heart?"

"Wow! I wasn't expecting that question. I thought I protected myself pretty well this morning," said Caroline. "Isn't it strange what happens when we bring the men into the picture?"

"They're not that complicated ladies," said Julia.

"No they're not. We are," said Diana. "Not to change the subject, but at some absurd pre-dawn hour this morning, a note and bag was left at our door. It was from Kate. In the bag was her gorgeous bridal bouquet with a note that said, *'We forgot to toss the bouquet last night! Please give it to the right woman or one of your daughters.'* So ladies, which of you is the right woman? Who will it be?"

"Well three of us are already very married," said Julia.

"And I feel like I just got a new husband," said Carmen, flashing her new ring.

Marti, Caroline and Sigrid looked at each other and back at the other three women.

"I don't think it's for me...Not me, not yet...I have no idea... You are not serious..."

"Okay my friends, let's just see what the next year will bring... For all of us."

The End

Book Club Topics & Queries

Scene 1 To Frank
Caroline still misses her husband terribly, and though he no longer appears to her, she occasionally senses his presence. Many women feel the presence of a lost loved one. Some tell stories of appearances, significant dreams, signs and coincidences. Do you have an experience you would be willing to share?

Scene 2 Reminiscence
Caroline's journals reflect a thoughtful, organized woman. She divides these journals between her ideas and plans and her private thoughts. This is one healthy outlet, when there is no one there to share your deepest feelings. How do you share your deepest feelings?

Scene 3 Nicole
Nicole's death was a great loss to many people, far beyond her immediate family. It's these senseless events that make us question everything we believe in. How do you deal with that which brings you to your knees?

Scene 4 Love in the Bakery
Sigrid's new business has brought her a greater sense of self. Her willingness to date again took great courage! Though her focus on business is not lost, she wants to bring him to meet her friends. Aren't you happy for her!

Scene 5 Adagio for Heartstrings
Another year went by and Marti did not find the courage to reveal to her son the truth about his father. One could say she sabotaged herself with her fear-based decisions. In one defining moment the two Eriks eyes met and they knew the truth. What did you think about the "reveal" at the concert?

Scene 6 – The Robles Predicament
Carmen and JB Robles have disagreements over money. What is it that money represents to JB? What does it represent to Carmen? Sensible Carmen seems to want to spend it and JB wants to save it. Do you relate?

Scene 7- Dinner is Served
The women take an evening to get current with each other and get real about the long road to "dream-come-true" status. The big surprise of the evening was the physical transformation of Sigrid! Okay – so who else wants a decade back? Would you? Have you? Come on ladies – your secret is safe!

Scene 8 – Diana's Triumphant Year
The return of Miss Elaina to the Greene ministry was an opportunity for Diana to stand up for what she believed in. This was a "Love Your Enemies" moment - Could you have done what she did?

Scene 9 – A Very Different Trip to the Mountain
In the AngelFire books the mountain is a metaphor for God. They go to the mountain for peace, inspiration, meditation and prayer. This time, they pay tribute to Nicole's life, by acknowledging her influence on each of their lives. We may not be aware

of how we affect each other's lives. Is there someone who has been a positive influence in your life that you might want to acknowledge?

Scene 10 – In the Meantime
The group ponders how they may have affected others along their own life path. Diana reminds them not to underestimate their influence on those they have met along the way. How would you want to be remembered by your friends?

Scene 11 – Showering Kate
As this intimate party unfolds, each woman creates a personal contribution to the pending wedding, instead of a traditional gift. In the midst of this lovely gathering the bride has made a fear-based decision to call the whole thing off! What did you think of Sigrid's speech? Would you have been willing to speak as honestly and directly to the bride regarding her decision? The scene move to the music room where once again these women sing together! Did you sing along with them?

Scene 12 – Reservations at Stonewood
As Robbie drowns his sorrows, JB joins him hoping for advice on how to straighten out his wife's spending problems. Instead, he receives an enlightening prosperity lesson. Did you agree with Robbie's summary?

Scene 13 – An Unexpected Guest
Caroline's ex-husband reappears. Where do you think this is going? Why?

Scene 14 – Our Blonde Bombshell
Sigrid has a new plan for her business! She wants to take a step up to the next level, and also wants to make Arturo a partner. Caroline is more skeptical than Robbie. Do you think she is making a wise business move or is it something more personal?

Scene 15 – Really, Caroline
It's a Spa Day! Diana attempts to discuss (without confrontation), the fact that Caroline has not yet embraced the fortune that Frank has left for her. In her grief, she has not been ready to create a new life for herself. How common is this? What would you have done with such a grand legacy?

Scene 16 – Who Knows What?
Caroline's concern about the Amoroso brothers seems to be handled with a little divine intervention, perhaps by Frank Amoroso himself. Have you recognized that kind of help when you need it?

Scene 17 – The Way We Were
A trip down memory lane creates laughter, with old photos from times gone by. Now that we live in the digital age, and in the advent of Facebook, will we ever lose those old photos? Will we ever live them down?

Scene 18 – Thank God It's Friday
Now we meet each of the families, who have gathered together to celebrate the wedding. JB has been invited to join the Robbie and the Amoroso brothers, for what promises to be quite an adventure! Is this a red flag?

Scene 19 - Truth Be Told
The mystery surrounding Nicole's death is beginning to unravel, which is painful for both Ric and Caroline. Their decision to keep the news to themselves until after the wedding was thoughtful – do you think they should have told Paula?

Scene 20 – The Family We Chose
The chosen family is sometimes easier to love than the ones we're born with – don't you agree? Which family members stand out the most for you?

Scene 21 – Breakfast for Twenty
The families mix and mingle and Caroline's sons asks for permission to finish Nicole's project. Could this help transform her grief?

Scene 22 – Chapel in the Woods
Could you visualize the beauty of this structure? JB and Robbie, will not be returning on time. Both Caroline and Carmen panicked – What do think happened?

Scene 23 – High Noon
We meet Sigrid's infamous daughter Sherri again, with quite the opposite behavior from Book I. When the mother changes, do the children change?

Scene 24 – Separate & Together
Paula arrives with her little band. The men arrive...The Groom, the Amoroso Brothers, and the newly refashioned JB....So what did you think of all the men of AngelFire?

Scene 25 – Let- All of Us - Eat Cake!
There is the wedding cake and Arturo. Which one do you think was more beautiful?

Scene 26 - Robles Revelations
What happened in Las Vegas, didn't stay in Las Vegas, for JB tells all! Was this a great prosperity lesson or a happiness lesson?

Scene 27 – A Natural Woman
The women gather to prepare the bride for the ceremony. Could you picture and appreciate their efforts?

Scene 28 – At Last, the Wedding – *Did you enjoy the service?*

Scene 29 – The Reception – *Did you enjoy the dinner, dancing, music?*

Scene 30 – After the Ball is Over
Moments of gratitude, goodbyes and Ric Robert's words of wisdom, regarding Caroline's future. Will it take a calling for Caroline to move on?

Scene 31 – Doors
Kate asks Diana to give the wedding bouquet to the right woman. Should it go to Caroline, Marti or Sigrid? Who do you think it could be?